mai

mai
silently mother

by

GEETANJALI SHREE

Translated from Hindi, with an Afterword, by

NITA KUMAR

NIYOGI
BOOKS

First published in Hindi as *Mai* by Rajkamal Prakashan, Delhi, in 1993.

Published by

NIYOGI BOOKS

D-78, Okhla Industrial Area, Phase-I
New Delhi-110 020, INDIA
Tel: 91-11-26816301, 49327000
Fax: 91-11-26810483, 26813830
email: niyogibooks@gmail.com
website: www.niyogibooksindia.com

The original Hindi © Geetanjali Shree
This translation © Nita Kumar

Layout: Shashi Bhushan Prasad
Cover design: Misha Oberoi
Cover illustration based on paintings by Paramjit Singh and Arpita Singh

ISBN: 978-81-933935-0-5

Publication: 2017

Printed at: Niyogi Offset Pvt. Ltd., New Delhi, India.

In my eagerness I fluttered my wings. Must not be mai,
must not be a prisoner, must not stay bent over.

Mai had shown me a bird in the sky who was trying so
hard to fly in one place. 'Look,' in that infinity of a sky
the bird was flapping its wings without going anywhere.
The whole sky was the bird's. But what use was it?
What use was an empty endless sky?

We always knew mother had a weak spine.
    The doctor told us that later.
That those who constantly bend get this problem. By bending all the time, the substance between the vertebrae gets eroded and the nerves get pressed here and there. That these people have pain all the time: pain when they bend, and pain when they stand up straight.

Mai was always bent over. We should know. We've been watching her from the beginning. Our beginning is her beginning after all. She was bent over right from the start, a silent spectre moving around, taking care of everyone's needs.

And there were plenty of people who had needs. People came to be in short supply in our house only later. At the time I am speaking of, the house was bustling, with family, with visitors, with servants and workers. Mai flitted between them, untangling and sorting out hundreds of threads.

The time was our childhood. The place was a huge house. We believed that everyone lived in such large houses. Langurs leaped around on the rooftops and we children could peep down through the ventilators. Peacocks called in the morning and later would decide to come down into the courtyard to dance. We collected their feathers from the fields and the rooftops, piles of them, to make odd things with. In the courtyard people would be coming and going, some that we chose to meet, some to hide from. Then, night, and the petromaxes burning.

Electricity came later. The hand pump too, a plaything for us. There were the iron and brass buckets in which mai or Hardeyi kept water from the hand pump for dadi, babu, or me. And there was a bell-metal tub in which Bhondu poured water for dada from the well every day.

Dada had his toilet and bathroom in a separate place—out in the front, next to his sitting room. It had a roof—but did it have a proper wall or was something propped up as a partition?—and a high, backless seat (not just a plank to squat on), a brass pot and the bell-metal tub. Brimming over with water. If dada had been forced to take a bath with a smaller quantity of water he might have given up bathing. On one side was a wooden commode that the sweeper emptied out every day.

Once we burst in by mistake from a game. Dada was cross-legged on the seat, water just poured over his head, the drops hanging on his sacred thread. He did not panic. He only said in a stern, curt voice, 'Out.' We left.

The rest of the family had their bathrooms inside, on the side of the verandah where dadi sat, facing the courtyard. The courtyard had the bathrooms on one side and the kitchen and wood and coal stores on the other. The hand pump was also in the courtyard. In the winter, Hardeyi made a wood fire to heat big pots of bathing water on. I can still see mai lifting the pots with the edge of her sari.

Later babu had one wall of their bedroom broken down and a new bathroom made with a flush, tap, shower, geyser, everything, even plastic buckets and mugs.

But that happened later. Many things had changed by that time. Dadi continued to bathe in the courtyard to the end—the tenacious thread that never broke—but almost everything else changed.

But all this was much, much later.

The trouble is that this voice itself is from 'much later', hopelessly consumed by the conviction that in the 'later' there is only memory. Memory, which is the past caught in an imaginary frame, not so much untrue as incomplete. The fear is not only that the story will be left half-told, but also that the story remains true only until it is captured in a frame. As soon as 'it' is held, 'it' will take on a new shape, become solid, a frozen part of history. Do we really want to gather all the things we find possible to say in this way, and deny the truth of the unsaid?

But the greater difficulty is that the story must be told. I cannot do anything else until I narrate mai.

I want to narrate 'mai' but the distance between 'mai' and the 'narration' is so troubled, so full of opposition, that one doesn't know how to cross that distance or what might happen on the way.

To find even a trace of 'mai', it is as if we have to enter a difficult fort. A fort complete with trapdoors, mazes, cellars, secret tunnels and puzzles. If we step ahead seeing light, we find ourselves falling screaming into a void. We creep carefully into a tunnel through its hidden door, confident of finding something on the other side, and find we have come back to where we started. We advance with some confidence that we are making progress and suddenly some hidden enemy pours boiling oil from a cauldron above.

How to reach 'mai'? How to get her out from this place after finding her? And the shards of mai we manage to get out, will they actually be her? Memory, time, the longing to understand might pierce her image through like a sieve. Mai is somewhere right now, whole, but when we catch her and bind her up in our words, she may be made half.

I don't know why this obsession with reviving mai arose. It is a desire that suffuses from the inside as well as the outside. It fills the lungs with breath and then begins to suffocate so that the breath has to be quickly expelled with a sigh. That mai, so weak from the very beginning, can fill someone up like this, is a shock.

But later. All this later.

Where it all begins—and now even this beginning might begin to shift and shake—was at a time before the later. At that time we were very small, dadi was very old, babu stayed out a lot, dada was very hot-tempered and mai was very scared. These were the people who populated, alone or in groups, our balloon-light, self-sufficient childhood.

There were grain fields and mango and guava orchards around the house in which workers laboured, whom we watched from afar. Today, if there are riots in the city, we know of them at least from the papers. But, back then, only dada knew of these workers and their problems. And if even babu was afraid of dada, how dare we little people ask anything?

Not that we just sat around or went around at all subdued. Old houses have their free and welcoming places. We could be hidden somewhere on the roof dreaming up stories. We could be at the well watching the bullocks doing their rounds irrigating the fields. We may not have been that good at climbing trees but we could certainly swing from some of the guava branches. And there was always something to get from the fields—we could be eating peas, scrunching *chana* greens, even pulling up the raw wheat grains to chew up. There were many ways to escape dada.

Our business with dada was limited anyway. He had no rest from his various get-togethers. He spent his whole day in his outside-facing sitting room. His food would be sent there, he would sleep there, every day visitors would gather there. His voice, however, would fill the whole house—roars of laughter, narrations, calls to the servants, sing-alongs with Fayaz Khan and Abdul Karim Khan.

—*Phulwan ki gaindan mein ka na maro re*
Mit piyarwa
—Don't hit me with flower balls,
Oh dear beloved—

And we would start up in a distant field or on the roof, and come running in to spy on him.

Dada kept playing his 78 RPM records on his trumpet style His Master's Voice gramophone till the day he died. His relationship with the rest of the house was simply one of intimidation. 'Is anyone there? Have something cold sent' (later, 'Who's there? Have some tea sent', though he did not take to drinking tea himself). 'Have some fritters made of pumpkin greens sent.'

'Is anyone around? Here are some sweets from the village, have some savouries sent to go with them.' It was dada's special style to say, not, 'Send', or 'Do.' But rather, 'Have it sent.' 'Have it done.'

Dada had no fixed time for his directions, but the single person they were aimed at was mai, who would swiftly set to work to fulfil his commands. If dada was the 'outside' and mai was the 'inside', then the bridges between them were Bhondu and Hardeyi. They were husband and wife, but Bhondu's estate extended over the outside, and Hardeyi's kingdom was the inside. At the boundaries, objects, messages, and scoldings were exchanged.

Apart from them—and us of course—there was only babu, who came and went between the inside and the outside. Inside to mai and dadi, then outside to dada in his sitting room. Babu would be tempted by his greed for music to sit with dada but would not be able to say anything beyond one-word sentences: 'Sir.' 'Right.' 'Of course.' 'Certainly.'

Everyone was afraid of dada. We never saw dadi with dada, perhaps not a single time—that was the kind of husband and wife they were. For dadi—with whom we were comparatively close—it was as if dada existed but not within her horizon. Maybe it was because it was only in dada's absence that her tongue could move with the speed and bitterness it did, so why should she acknowledge the existence of a speedbreaker? She would sit the whole day in the inside verandah on a large bed with a white sheet and much-washed blue bolster pillow, reigning like a queen. In front of her were the courtyard and kitchen with all their activities. Every separate room opened into the verandah and her eyes and ears would be immediately trained in the direction of any sound. Dadi, fresh from her bath, her white hair spread out, spectacles on her nose. Her tongue working busily in her hollow cheeks, moving her head swiftly this side or that, keeping track of every comer.

We had no restrictions on inside and outside in those early days, but in dada's sitting room we did not even have an interest. If dada saw us running past he would say in a strict voice, 'O Subodh, wait a minute,' and pull us toward him and put us in his lap with his arms around us like a boa about to crush our bones to pieces. Or he would poke us with his *'Ala bala garam masala'*, tease us with *'Akkar bakkar bombay bo'* or simply stretch out his hands, 'Here, crack my fingers.' We would shriek and twist, but finally run away only when he let us go, with the feeling that even if we had had no fun, it was no small matter that such a grand personage had held us on his lap.

But for the most part we had little to do with the men, a lot to do with the women. When not busy with ourselves outside, it was not dada or babu that we hovered around, but dadi and mai. We became dadi's favourites, but our own favourite became mai. Such a favourite that all the energy of our childhood began to be gathered up in one aim: how to rescue and take her away.

Her helplessness hurt us even in our early childhood. Slowly, we began to rescue her from everyone—from dadi, from babu, from dada. But we could not save her from herself. When her spine failed her, the doctor also declared defeat. She would always be in pain, he said. We of course had known about this problem of hers with her backbone from the very beginning. The rest was later.

Mai was always bent over. And said little.

When we opened our eyes in the morning she would be freshly bathed, in a clean cotton sari, making *parathas* in the kitchen. Parathas of peas, grams, lentils. Or potatoes, cauliflower, radishes. Dada and dadi did not have breakfast, they straightaway had a full lunch. Whatever was made for them would be packed for our school snack. But babu had a light meal in the morning. A handful of five grains—wheat, peanuts, gram, masur and moong lentils—soaked together and sprouted. Mai sprinkled salt and lemon juice on them and served them to babu with a large glass of buttermilk.

Fresh buttermilk was made at home almost everyday. A wooden churner worked in a large clay pot. Sitting on a low stool in the courtyard, holding the pot between her heels, mai would make the curds and the butter jump and churn. Then the butter floated on top and the buttermilk was served around in large glasses.

Every job that was done by mai was also done by Hardeyi. There was no clear separation between jobs that were only mai's and those that were only Hardeyi's. Sometimes mai churned the buttermilk and sometimes Hardeyi. Sometimes mai ground the chutney or lentils and sometimes Hardeyi. Sometimes mai brought in the wood and lit the stove and sometimes Hardeyi. True, mai almost always did the cooking and Hardeyi the sweeping and mopping of the rooms. After that, Hardeyi hardly went inside and kept hovering around the verandah and courtyard with mai.

The thing was that dada did not like servants inside the house. Apart from the fear of theft, if they were given the freedom to move around they might become bold enough to talk back. He was also worried that news of the 'inside' would travel to the 'outside'. Besides, the 'class' of servants spreads disease. So although we had a water carrier, a sweeper, a gardener, a watchman and other such servants living on the compound, the only ones allowed inside the house—with restrictions—were Hardeyi and Bhondu. Bhondu looked after the work of the outer verandah and dada's sitting room and transacted with Hardeyi at the back. When approaching dada he took off his slippers and wore his cap. His respect for his master's standards of cleanliness made him keep his hair close cropped. And Hardeyi helped out inside.

With mai.

Mai who did every job bent down—the washing, the grinding, the rolling, the baking.

It seemed that in our house there was always a celebration of eating. Dada and dadi could have only fresh, steaming food. Babu had weak digestion and also had to be served not by Hardeyi's dirty hands but only by mai's. And we were no less demanding—full of our careless childhood plus some of our own more original demands.

Mai was versatile in her cooking. Could it always have been so? For dada and dadi the orthodox fried foods—puris, parathas (dadi preferred puris because she wanted to eat light and puris are so light they balloon up to the top of the pan), fried vegetables, cream, and rice pudding made orthodox with two drops of ghee. For babu and us dal or curry, *roti*, rice, vegetables, salad. For everyone, *papads*, chutney, yoghurt, pickles. And sometimes just like that, perhaps at someone's visit, dada or dadi's command, or a monsoon downpour, fritters, fries, pancakes, halwa, were ladled out by the trayful. Babu was a careful eater. He might taste the 'light' puris or fritters, but he survived on cottage cheese and honey, buttermilk and sprouted grain. Later, we were responsible for the introduction of new, Western things, some of which babu ate with pleasure and all of which dadi always did—soup cutlets, sandwiches, ice cream, cake, biscuits, chocolate.

That is to say, there were many types of menus in that one house. The whole range from London to our neighbouring village flourished in our kitchen. That is what we were raised on. It's not easy to forget. Both cake and *gur* have gone into our making. Maybe we are cross-breeds, spotted, some wild exotic plant. But that's us.

So we blossomed under many shadows. But most of all, mai's. And yet were so senseless of the reality behind that shadow.

For a long time we had no idea when mai arose in the morning, what she ever ate, how she existed. When we began to give it a thought was when we began to feel love and pity. Our separate demands stopped, like: 'Today, mai, I really feel like having *batis*,' or: 'Make *littis*!', or: 'It's so long since I had *gulgules*.' We even started interfering in others' food habits. Subodh would pull mai out of the kitchen, 'Enough, now stop, come out immediately... out of there...*I'll* turn them over.' I tried to help her too. And old habits died, such as the sitting with dadi and gobbling up food, with mai serving. Instead: 'No, we'll wait until you come...let it get cold...' Further, as a student of science, I began to lecture dadi and babu about diet, what our body needed, how to avoid fried foods, cut down on the sweets and things that caused stomach problems and were injurious to teeth. Everyone except dada—I never managed to tell him anything. For a long time.

Dada and dadi were at the peak of their reigns—one on a throne in the outer sitting room, the other on the inner verandah. In dada's time there were baskets of sweets in the house—spherical laddus of sesame seeds, spices, and parched rice from the village, round and diamond-shaped milk sweets from the sweetseller in the bazaar. No fruits were bought from the market until much later, on our insistence. Our home-grown guavas, papayas, bananas, *jamun*, berries, custard apples were there for everyone all the time—us, the servants, the birds. They were not included in treats.

But there was one fruit that outdid every fruit in the world when it was in season—mangoes. In our home we had unlimited langras, dasehris, chausas, and local sucking mangoes.

Even dada had nothing against mangoes. It was sweets, however, that he really tucked into. He ate strictly deep fried and syrupy sweet things. He never went for a walk. He had lost one tooth in all, between the ages of seventy and eighty. 'Look at my teeth, look at my digestion, and keep your science to yourself,' he would tell me off.

Dada did try going for a walk one day with seven or eight other old men. One had indigestion, one had a backache, another had pain in the joints, yet another suffered from insomnia—all of them had given up on life. Dada asked each in turn, 'How long have you been going for this morning walk, my dear?' One said ten years, another, twenty, a third that it was now five years that he was building up his health. So our dada told them adieu. 'You are welcome to your salubrious morning walk. You won't find me here from the morning.' Dada's walk continued as before: from the verandah to the sitting room, from the sitting room to the verandah.

Dadi was a food buff. It was this common passion that must have been a strong bond between her and dada—if there had been one at all. She continued to demand steaming hot, spicy, rich foods. When she lost all her teeth she simply crushed the food into powder and then dispatched it.

We had learnt some nutrition-related facts and asked for boiled porridge, at which dadi scolded mai, 'Feeding them *raw* porridge... as if by frying it a little you'll go bankrupt...'

Mai replied softly that it wasn't raw and the children did not want it fried.

But could anything keep dadi quiet?—'Huh, the children want...a great excuse for laziness.'

We were quite old at that point. 'Dadi, this is eaten all over the West without being fried.'

Dadi spat fire. 'That's what you all are being made into—Englishmen. The more tight-fistedness in this house, the whiter your skin will become.'

Subodh spoke up. 'Why are you always after mai, always insulting her. Tell us whatever you have to say. *We* had asked mai for the porridge.'

Dadi's eyes popped out. 'See, see, this is the way of Englishmen, not to show any respect for anyone.'

Subodh exploded, 'All of you show a lot of respect for mai, don't you?'

'Wonderful,' said dadi swaying, 'I suppose I have to wash her feet and drink the water?'

Mai, worried, tried to hush us up. 'Quiet, shhh...shhh...that's enough...now be quiet...'

'That's what you always teach,' Subodh attacked her now, 'that we should be quiet and accept everything.'

He was getting into the habit of losing his temper.

We did not want to be quiet like mai. Head down, eyes on the ground, listening to others, doing as others wanted.

Although this was the only thing about mai that even dadi appreciated. Mai had at least this virtue for which she was forgiven all her other shortcomings—that the whole day passed and daughter-in-law's voice was not heard even once, that even when she went to the club her head was covered with her sari. Dadi was told, 'Mataji, it is because of your good deeds that you got a humble, simple, sweet daughter-in-law like her who never raises her eyes.'

Dadi would teach me, 'Child, this is the real parda.'

So powerful was dadi's will that mai was in 'parda' all day long.

Then it would be evening and long shadows fell on the trees and we came in from playing to find mai waiting for us with glasses of fresh tomato juice. Helping us to wash our hands and feet, rubbing rosewater and glycerine on them, feeding others and us, she would finally come into our room with us.

Our room, hers and ours.

Mai did not live in babu's room though she went there at night. We knew this because we didn't like it. We were afraid for her and we would call out, call her to come back.

Then in our room mai would slowly remove her 'real parda'.

How the three of us would laugh in that room! It was as if we were three children of the same age. Mai spent much of her time checking our home-work, although babu told someone in the club with a laugh once that they shouldn't ask her about our home-work, they should ask some educated person. When we accosted mai with that she told us she was an FA (First Arts) pass. In our room we were not shy about anything. We giggled all the time.

Then mai would tell us stories and jokes in bed. Sahab said to the gardener, 'Why don't you water the plants?' The gardener said, 'Sahab, it is raining.' The sahab scolded him, 'Use an umbrella.' When the driver stopped the car the sahab asked, 'What happened?' The driver told him, 'Sahab, there is a pit ahead of us.' The sahab ordered, 'Blow the horn.'

All the sahabs in mai's stories were fools. And in her longer stories, the poor people who were considered fools turned out victorious.

Helplessness was a victory in itself. We had concluded that, but did not think about it.

Not that we did not give it a thought then, but we learnt to think about our thoughts only later. That is why, earlier, mutually contradictory thoughts co-existed quite harmoniously and happily within us. They did not ask tense questions of each other, or seek their truth in one another. We simply observed that if babu so much as raised his eyes, mai withdrew like a lamb behind the door and we came forward to save the 'poor' thing. In the very next moment she would receive the challenge of someone's eyes raised at us in such a way that babu or dada, whoever it was, would retreat and we would unhesitatingly hide ourselves behind her.

When we began to think of our thoughts, then questions came at us from all sides. Who was the 'poor' thing? Who saved whom...? Every answer bred a new, scorpion-like attack. Such stinging attacks that there was neither an antidote for the poison, nor a quick end, only a lasting pain and a confused, dizzy head. Mai...mai...mai...?...?...?...?

Dadi used to say that mai had only one virtue—her parda. That was the parda that made us cry. Whatever may happen and come to pass, parda was inexcusable. Indefensible. And dadi accepted as much, in a bitter voice—'Why, parda today is the name only of that thing which is hung on doors and windows.'

But the surprise lies in something else. That when we saw a parda on a door or window we knew well that behind it lay a fully arranged room. A home, where everything was in place according to someone's wishes. We may have even idly wondered at a curtain seen in a new place—what is behind this? Never did we think that there was only that parda in a silence, with nothing before it and behind it. Never did we believe that it flapped in a void.

But looking at mai's parda we forgot there was something behind it as well.

The parda that was the seal of mai's modesty and forbearance. Mai, the shadow incarnate who listened to everyone, served everyone.

Listened even to dadi, who talked as if looks, manners, skill, intellect, even a mother's love, had become extinct with her generation and not evolved any further.

Dadi could not be bullied by anyone. The one from whom she may have taken it had broken away from her. Fair, with brown eyes, she gloried in her looks till the end. She would point to mai and say—'She is young, and look at her! By the time she is my age, she will have no looks at all! I am fairer than her even today!' She waved her arms in the air to demonstrate. 'Because of her Sunaina is so dark. Now, my darling son has taken after me. He used to look like an Englishman.'

The funny thing was that she never called Subodh dark and when as a child I complained at this, she giggled in a masterly way with her hollow mouth—'Hee hee...He goes out in the sun, naturally his colour is already gone. Anyway he is a boy after all. A *laddu* made of ghee may be crooked, but remains a laddu, hee hee...'

She would take my hands in hers and say—'Now, see, the way your veins stick out at this age? Why, my hands were so soft and silky that if anyone touched them they would want to keep touching them.'

Then she would narrate how in her youth some English friend of dada's told him that his missis had such beautiful hands and feet, he (the Englishman) was going to shake hands with her one day, whether dada liked it or not. When dadi's first son was born—dadi

gave birth to eleven children but only babu and one sister survived—
the Englishman gave his congratulations and quickly picked up her
creamy hands and held them in his own for a few moments.

It was true that dadi's movements, even in her old age, had a
certain attitude. When she stood still and talked her waist would
be bent jauntily to one side, both hands joined behind her head
with grace, shoulders swaying, head at an angle, and a dagger of
a glance sent forth!

However, dadi had always been old. When she spoke of her
youth, she possibly spoke about another life. Yes, when she walked
straight she was less old, and when she began to limp, she was older.

She had been sitting down one time, stood up, and fell down
flat. Her foot had been asleep and she had not realised it. Her
fall broke the bones of her hip joint into pieces. Her bones had
become crisp like dry tinder in old age.

Dadi screamed and wept, so that even dada pushed all his
hatred of doctors aside and sent babu running between home and
hospital like a whirlwind in a closed room—this way, that way, that
way, this way.

The affair became bigger and reached Lucknow. Babu and
the compounder together lifted dadi, put her in someone's car for
the station, and whisked her straight through on a train onto the
operation table of the most magnificent hospital in Lucknow.

We were also there. Our first time in a city, first time on a
train. It was the height of summer and dadi angrily hid every
limb behind her sheets, every part of her body, as if there was
a diamond here and a pearl there and they might roll away. An
England-returned doctor threw away the shattered bone and
replaced it with an imported, top quality joint. Then dadi started
walking, with a limp.

Most of the time she sat on the verandah resting against her
blue bolster pillow. On winter evenings huge canvas curtains
would be pulled down and on summer afternoons *chik* bamboo

curtains and she would sleep. Her body properly covered. We all congregated there, whiling our time away. All except dada, whom dadi would never meet.

Mai would also come but not to while away her time. She'd come to ask something, to do something, take the keys, press her legs, or oil her hair. She respected every order of dadi's.

Dadi loved to eat, and in matters of food was neither traditional nor orthodox. She would get mai to make *kachauris*—'This way...do that...fill them like this...' Early in the morning she had Hardeyi tell Bhondu—'Get fresh *jalebis and samosas*.' We would be given some too. And in the evening Bhondu would be sent running for *chat*.

The other things that were introduced thanks to us were equally beloved of dadi. For instance, she would dunk her bread into condensed milk to soften it, and gobble it up.

We had replaced one cuisine with another. We wanted one thing only, for instance stew, and that would be a full meal for us. But she kept up with one cuisine and merely added another to it. The first was for nourishment and satisfaction of hunger, the second for the greater pleasures of the tongue. Diversity is the charm of life! We who had started off to make mai's work lighter ended up increasing it. Mai would be making something or the other all the time. And thanks to dadi, the things that needed ghee—like halwa—got tons of it, and the things that did not need ghee at all—like chana and *lai*—were also roasted in ghee.

Whether her stomach accepted it or not, dadi observed no restraints in matters of diet. The doctor warned her a thousand times, but dadi remained true to herself. Yes, she would do as much as to serve herself a touch of vegetables and a tiny piece of roti before others, saying—'Here, now don't tell me I don't listen to the doctor. Let's see if this saves my life.'

Mai would pick up a bowl to serve seconds—'Some more?' and dadi's hollow mouth would tremble in self-pity—'Some more

what? Everything is forbidden. Now I must just lie around without
food. Like a ripe mango that can fall anytime, who knows when?'

And then quietly, with her limp, she would find her way to the
kitchen to lick some cream with sugar, or powder some nuts to
swallow them.

Most of all, even when dadi would be sitting eating away, if
she got in the mood to weep over her fate, she would start—

'Now, I have hardly even tasted anything, but this doctor is
after me, don't eat this, don't eat that, eat less. So I am eating less,
and what miracle do we see?'

Anyway, we stopped making our separate demands and
gradually became the proponents of a less showy but healthier
diet. Dadi never liked or understood this. She would say constantly
that this was nothing but mai's laziness. She never tired of
elaborating on how she herself had given incomparable service
to her mother-in-law. Toothless, her mother-in-law had once said,
'Oh, *bahu*, I know it's out of the question, but in the rains doesn't
one go mad for corn!'

And dadi had replied, 'You *will* have corn, mother, you will.'

She had gone and picked a soft ear from the field, roasted it
mildly, took out the pieces, mashed them lovingly, mixed in some
spices, and fed it to her mother-in-law with her own hands.

Her mother-in-law was touched to the core. 'Bahu, you did
feed me corn after all.'

'If I make up my mind to do something, I can do it,' was her
refrain. 'I can even learn English.'

But she rarely made up her mind to do anything. Even if mai
had a headache it was mai who did all the work. Later I began to
do some, and Subodh to try some. But dadi? She remained her
beautiful, eloquent, gourmet self.

Mai did all the work and dadi made all the comments. Not
directly critical, but oblique and indirect. 'Is this what is called *khir*
in today's day and age?'

We: 'Ah, mai, the khir is wonderful!'

She: 'All right, all right, you can call it good in a sort of way. The milk is good, the rice is good, even if eaten separately they would taste good. Yes, in my time we believed in thickening it well. Then the milk and rice would become one in the khir. But what a waste of time, what a waste of milk, you sweat in front of the fire for hours...that was the khir my mother-in-law ate.'

Subodh said, 'Dadi, that's why your mother-in-law died early.'

But dadi's shafts got ever sharper. If babu was around they had a special edge to them.

'This boy grew up licking his fingers after eating *rabri*. See if you can do that. Or get satisfaction from just licking your fingers.'

Or: 'Well, what a great thing. You kept the squash close to raw and saved yourself a lot of vitamins.'

It was we who had lectured once that too much cooking spoiled the 'nutritional value' of the thing. Now mai could not say anything, and in any case she would not say anything.

Dadi's shots were such that no one could say for sure that they were meant to hurt. If the rice stayed moist—'See here, in our part of the world any shortcoming can be taken care of at one stroke. Here you have boiled rice as well as *khichri*.' Her voice was innocent. Was it cold satire or a thoughtful taking of mai's side before anyone else could criticise her?

Once she said—'Did you boil the *suji* today, bahu? That's a great trick! It gets cooked, the milk gets saved, you put a touch of milk on top and you're all set. No, I'm serious. The way I used to make it the suji drank up all the milk. Certainly the taste was different, but if you haven't tasted that, you'll like this fine.' She looked at us as if issuing a challenge: go ahead, say something! But am I criticising your mai, or am I instead admitting that she has taught me something new? She looked at babu lovingly and smiled. Babu was unable to react and gurgled an artificial laugh.

She was crazy about babu. She narrated thousands of times how her son was more handsome than nawabs and rajahs. He could have women flat before him like flies and mosquitoes sprayed with Flit.

'...He could have got an angel, that boy, but...' she would give a long sigh—'fate does not always play fair.' Mai would be right there, busy at something. Silent. '...Who knows the work of the Lord? Some people get everything they want without trying. They come with empty hands and start bathing in milk and honey.'

Every month or two dadi would have pain all over her body. In the day she would swallow the powder that dada sent in. In the evening she would move mai aside and make space for babu. Then she would moan and thrash her limbs about. She would grip babu's hands and cry. Babu would massage her whole body—head, waist, legs. Dadi would bless him—may everyone have such a son. She would rest her head against him, wrap herself around him. She would be in such agony that whenever, later, we saw a woman in labour in a film we always remembered her. Babu would be pressing her legs, from ankle to knee, and she would be stretched flat out crying—'More...harder...oh god...a little higher...'

Babu was reputed to be like a mythological Videha or a Janak, happy in all circumstances, content in spite of any deprivation. Babu never dreamt of conquering Mt Everest, or harboured any ambition of crossing the seas. Somehow he completed his studies, got a diploma in engineering and on the basis of dada's contacts, got a job in one of the industrial complexes in the city. He went to work by scooter every day and came back by scooter. Having left in the morning, he was expected back any time in the evening. He would rest a bit in his room, sit by dadi a little, maybe go into dada's sitting room, and then at any moment leave the house. He would often return late.

There was a place called 'The Club' behind our house. It existed thanks to the saheb-like aspirations of the businessmen and bureaucrats of our small town. It had a billiard room and a card room. Babu went there to play cards. On festivals and New Year's Day there was a fete at the Club, and then mai would also go. On foot with us, through the fields at the back, climbing over the boundary wire. After dada and dadi died, mai went more often, but earlier it was only babu who hung around the Club.

What drew babu to dada's sitting room was not dada's company but the music. Not only did dada deliver monologues rather than converse, babu was himself a poor speaker. Even his voice was hang-dog. He gave instructions to mai that were inaudible. Mai, of course, attended to all of them. Babu would even tell mai what he had to tell us, and do so in the same tired, worn-out voice.

However, later we understood that, just like clubs, dictatorship also comes in many shapes. One had a grand bearing and seemed fiercely cruel; another acted innocent, and seemed simple and weak.

The truth is that whatever babu ever said to mai he said softly, in a few words. If there was a feast or a celebration he took her out. And after dada and dadi, when there came the era of his involvement in affairs of the home, he bought every gadget for her. He was never asked. He did it himself, with pleasure. Gas, cooker, heater, geyser, even a washing machine. A fridge had already come during dada's time because somehow dada had let it. Babu kept bringing more things. When he went out of town he brought a sari and sweater for mai, clothes and toys for us.

But throughout there was a feeling of 'so what?...'. Maybe it was the keeping silent at dadi's antics, or even smiling with her at her nasty digs. Or regularly turning his eyes away to get lost in himself. We were never quite sure when he was at home and when not. Everyone else's life was bound by rules or even a sort of imprisonment, only he was like a pigeon among them all, hopping in all directions, feeble like a pigeon, free like a pigeon. With no problem of ever having to answer to anyone.

Babu was a firm devotee. He did his puja daily. Mai cleaned up the puja room early in the morning—including making the lamp, the wick, a Shiva lingam out of wet clay—and got the flowers ready. Babu arrived, sat cross-legged, naked except for a *dhoti*, lit the lamp and incense, offered individual flowers at each deity's feet, sprinkled Ganga water with a mango leaf on each icon and picture, put vermilion, murmured a prayer, rotated the light, and then left asking us to take the leavings from inside. We would run to get the consecrated sweet, then put it to our forehead.

In the winter babu's bath water was kept in the sun in the courtyard. He bathed there at the handpump, his sacred thread shivering, singing between chattering teeth at each helping of water:

—Wash your head, you meet the Lord
Wash your ears, you find God
Wash your neck, you get Krishna
Wash your chest, you reach Kashi

In short, God lived everywhere, from head to foot.

There were pujas at festivals too. There were *katha* narrations occasionally in the house. Fasts were frequent, almost all kept by mai. But babu kept the *navratri* fast and when it was over he heard its katha and did puja and ate prasad.

Babu was also hung up on saints, mystics, and astrologers. He was so superstitious that if he was leaving for office and Subodh asked, 'Babu, where are you going? Be sure to get my book today,' he stopped at the gate. 'Darn you, you stopped me.' He turned his scooter back, asked for a glass of water, and then set out again. In the same way, if a cat crossed his path he would turn his scooter around and take a longer route to work, or spit 'thu-thu-thu-thu' on the cat-crossed road. If he happened to sneeze, he would stop whatever he was doing for a while. Something like this would go on all the time.

Later, babu became a disciple of Turiyatit Baba and left *pan*, tobacco, alcohol, tea, eggs, onions, garlic, vinegar, and so on. On his way back from Baba's ashram, at night, his rickshaw would crunch on the gravel in the driveway.

The rickshawalla would start complaining—'Saheb, it's late at night. Even during the day it is five rupees from the station.'

But babu could never stop bargaining for an anna or two or abusing rickshawallas and such. 'Go off, you crook, whom do you think you can cheat? It's only two rupees during the day. Is this my first time? There is a police post nearby, do you want me to send you there, you dishonest fool? Even the three rupees is more than the rule, take it if you like, or just go.'

Babu would enter the house grumbling.

Enter and sit down near dadi. His eyes would be filled with humble devotion, his head with Baba's charismatic personality.

'Baba is no ordinary person. He is god himself, ammaji. The first day I saw him only from afar, the second day he turned and looked directly at me...I was struck by a "current"... The third day he passed by me, so I bent down and had hardly touched his feet when...flash! Like electricity...ammaji, he has such power...such charisma.'

Turiyatit Baba had many devotees. There were hundreds of stories about his powers, how the disabled started walking, the dead came alive, and so on. People would hang his picture in their puja room. Babu too hung up his pictures, big and small, on his scooter, in his bedroom, his puja room, his office. He would hand around packets of the holy ashes from Baba's ashram.

There were stories that the ashes appeared magically everyday under the pillow of one great devotee. In another's home they appeared in the shape of an 'Om' on fresh yogurt. Then it happened that in our home too a black dust was found scattered right near his hand in Baba's picture. Babu was delighted. When Subodh opened the frame and announced, 'It's mould,' only mai smiled quietly.

Babu had a good knowledge of the Hindu scriptures and now and then narrated some part of one of them to dadi. Dadi herself regularly recited an odd verse of Tulsidas or sang a composition by Sur or Rahim. Nor did she tire of complaining that mai was never to be found reading or reciting anything good, and that children unfortunately turn out like their mothers.

It was babu's belief that the Hindu dharma was the source of wisdom of the whole universe and of all its philosophy and beliefs. Before the language of the English had come into being there was already in the *Ramcharitmanas, 'Near avan'* or 'Come here'. First there was our goddess Girija, then came the *girijaghar* or church. The Bible says 'Om' all the time, such as where God says 'I om that I om' which because of mis-pronunciation came to be 'I am that I am'. Babu also told us that Turiyatit Baba himself was mentioned in the Bible, that Baba was himself Jesus, and the proof of this was that when Jesus said, 'I shall come again,' the sheep said 'Ba-ba'.

But if in religious matters babu considered the English lowly, in matters of civility he wanted to imitate them. After dada and dadi's death it was he who brought into the house a dining table and chairs, napkins, knives and forks. It was he who was proud of Subodh's English. For me he wanted that, yes, I should stay within the bounds of modesty, but in jeans or a dress.

Similarly, babu loved our own music, but he was not averse to Western bands and instruments. He may not have played them himself, but he had no objection to Subodh playing them. On his return from the hostel Subodh taught me the twist—babu watched appreciatively and even bent his knees and swayed slightly himself. But if by chance we played Hindi folk music or film songs on the radio, then without saying a word, he would just turn it off as if we were not there. We would also keep quiet. We always turned on the radio after carefully looking around, and turned it off on recognising babu's footsteps.

He only gave up this habit when I too left for the hostel. The trouble was that by then my appetite for film music was more or less satiated.

It was never easy to argue with babu. What was the point of a one-sided argument, as he hardly spoke? He stayed comfortably within himself. He came to dadi, rubbed the soles of her feet with oil if they were causing pain, sat with his head bent by dada's side, maybe said little affectionate things to us which we couldn't particularly remember, and handed mai bundles of things for us. Thanks to him mai left her coal stove and began to make rotis on a gas stove, the taste of which displeased our ungrateful family for ages. Just like we couldn't get the proper taste of lentils-cooked-in-a-brass-pot when they came to be done in a pressure cooker. But mai did get some respite, and got it thanks to babu.

Only mai, however. Nothing like that happened to Hardeyi. Even after the arrival of the washing machine, Hardeyi beat up and washed half the pile of clothes. Mai herself asked for a high sink in the kitchen so that Hardeyi could wash the dishes more easily, but babu did not remember. Hardeyi always sat on the ground on a wooden board, scrubbing the pots and pans from a stream of water falling from a high tap to which she had attached a piece of cloth.

Thus passed mai's time with babu. His fussiness—special food, preparations for bathing and puja—was carefully nurtured by mai. Babu would come in from somewhere, walk onto the carpet in his room, unbutton his outside pants and shirt, and step out of them so cleanly that his shape still remained in the clothes. Mai would come, pick up the clothes, empty them of his form and either hang them up for the next day or remove them for washing.

It was not possible to quarrel with babu. We wanted mai to fight with him, but no matter how much we encouraged her, she never did. Nor did mai mention that other woman. Nor did we dare ask her. We only knew from a night-time whispering that babu had taken this woman to Lucknow. Later, Subodh parked the scooter in front of her house in the dark—'That's her.' And I still could not believe it, even after I recognised babu's sweater, hand-knitted by mai, inside the house.

Maybe I did not want to believe it. But it could be something else too. I believed a bad woman was one whose body bulged like an overripe mango, whose tight sari made her thighs slobber as she walked and on whose back, under her high blouse, tyres of obscene flesh oozed sexuality.

Like the head-mistress who visited dada.

Dada's princely habits were the pride of our house. Dada had, in fact, been a landlord. He had given up his property in the fervour of Gandhi's non-cooperation movement. He wrote it off in babu's name. Then passed the age of eighty on the pension of a freedom fighter.

He loved music, loved hospitality, loved poetry, loved riding—there was no princely passion he did not have. Tall and well built, with a voice as resounding as the sky, and moustaches that you could swing on. His dress was a dhoti with an embroidered border, topped with a starched homespun kurta, and a severely folded embroidered shawl on his shoulder. In the winter he wore *khadi* silk.

Dada was famous in the whole town. His death was covered in the papers—'Freedom fighter passes away, leaves behind an only son and rest of the family.' I wondered, why the only daughter, our bua, was swallowed up in the 'rest of the family'. Anyway, he died old. Before that he was a grand, fearless old man whose stature permitted him to tell off even the English. He had a few English friends with whom he went for shikar or riding, but he was never bettered by them.

But these things were from a time with which we kept no contact. By the time we began to notice things, dada was having his get-togethers in his sitting room. With its old carved couch and armchairs, carpets, spittoons, the seat on which dada sat, and a huge bolster pillow. On the wall hung two pictures of dada himself, in

ivory frames. In one he stood straight and stiff in his coat-tails with a
pipe in his hand and an Alsatian by his side. In the other he sat, but so
stiffly that it seemed there were three parts of him glued together—
one from his feet to his knees, one from knees to waist, and the third
from waist to his head. His palms were kept straight, symmetrically
on the right and left thighs as if they were plates on a table.

Apart from this his sitting room had all the paraphernalia of
his music. And his hangers-on.

Dada had no friends, he had hangers-on. That is why it was
only his booming voice that could ever be heard. In return for their
silent, appreciative presence, his courtiers were given, again and
again, drinks, snacks, and tea.

This was the programme for the whole day. Dada would shout
his order, Bhondu would reach Hardeyi from the back door of the
courtyard, mai would quickly set out the ordered dishes on a tray
in Hardeyi's hands, and it would travel back. Sometimes this chain
would continue till midnight, especially the drinks and tea.

Dada himself did not drink tea. Only an elixir made from
boiling seven basil leaves in milk, morning and night. He was
then safe from mosquito bites, and he had no fear of malaria or
filaria. He drank various juices the rest of the day—of lemon,
berry, and watermelon.

It would seem that dada had no knowledge of or interest in
what was happening in the house. But in fact he was the know-
all and he could take an interest at any time, even hearing things
that had never been spoken. There was no question of his desires
being thwarted or anything being done against his wishes. If he
called ants elephants, that was fine. If he called kicks love, so be it.
If he gave an order the whole house stood at attention. Maybe he
was lost in a thought, and said by mistake—'I'll eat rice and spicy
peppered peas today.' And mai would push aside her whole cooked
meal and begin again. We did not even have a fridge then. Dada
made his dislike of most of these foreign gadgets clear.

Secondly, he disliked women. He did not want any females to be seen in the front part of the house. I remember there were berry bushes along the gravel path from the gate to the house. We were always picking on those purple, sometimes raw green, seeds. There would be the sound of the gate opening. Without bothering to check who had come, dada would say, 'Go inside Sunaina, ask them to send some refreshments.' At that moment I could see the woman in myself.

Dadi, mai, Hardeyi, no woman went out in front of him. We could only wonder, has dada ever seen a woman or not?

But that headmistress arrived and someone chased me inside. Dadi was resting, mai was massaging her and dadi kept muttering about the falsity and lowness of womankind. Then she began to abuse mai.

'Gave me a bad coin, that's what they did. My poor son...'

Mai did not say a word, just went away, and returned in a while with a bottle of oil and began to oil dadi's hair.

They had jointly made up some excuse so that we could not leave the courtyard. But even without knowing much, the little we understood made us find a chance to reach the roof. From up there we had seen the oily, shiny, buffalo-like woman, a beaded purse swinging in her hand, the obscene flesh on her chest shaking. She walked ahead and behind her was a young man, perhaps her son.

We did not understand anything and then came the age when we understood even what did not exist. And after that came the age when it seemed sheer melodrama to 'understand' everything. All these phases of understanding got so entangled that now it is impossible to find one balanced viewpoint to fix on. Is it not melodramatic to 'understand'? Is it real to not understand? This is so difficult. Only now and then, just like that, the vision of that boy with his face down, walking behind that woman, flashes by. Was there a shade of some familiar face on his face? Some floating

shadow from our home that had fallen on his? Part of a nose, or
lip, or something else, from one of us?

Can it ever happen like that? Can someone perish after
having been nameless, unknown, and no one aware that a written
word existed and is now totally erased? If you bury a tale forever,
will it not trip up someone sometime and make itself heard? If
someone starts digging there by chance, will it not blurt out
its story?

This is so frightening. To put someone beyond death, and make
him nameless, invisible. To empty someone into non-existence.

When does one ever put up a curtain in an empty room? On
our part we did something too to contribute to so many stories
remaining untold, being buried unceremoniously. As if they had
never existed.

We had scolded mai that she let dadi say all that she did. Mai
told me that dadi's bald spot was not from old age. Dadi used to
hide in the storeroom when dada was drunk and he would pull her
out by the hair. Mai said that dadi's and her *jati* was the same and
she could not turn away from her own kind. And I experience a
strange weakness in finding the reflections of both these women
in myself. I cannot blame them whose face and body can clearly be
glimpsed in my own.

The headmistress had met dada in his sitting room. There was
a time when she would come. There was a time when she never
came again.

The life of the house continued according to its rules. Dada,
his eyes closed, waving his hands with pleasure, kept enjoying his
music. But none of the rest of us was free to sing or to dance. He
was in his bath one day and mai passed by humming something.
He immediately came out and opened the door from his sitting
room to the courtyard. Mai quickly covered her head and stood
to one side—

'Who was singing? Was someone singing?'

That was all and he disappeared without waiting for an answer. I can swear that mai never ever hummed again.

The dilemma was that we were both ready to learn music and dance. Subodh began to go to guitar classes in his school. There was nothing like that in my school. Apart from regular classes there was one subject, Home Science—cooking, sewing, knitting—in which I was not interested. I got after mai and she spoke to Nagji Appa's sister in the club and arranged for her daughter's teacher, Ustad Nanhe Khan, to come to our house to teach me dance. He would have to climb over the barbed wire at the back and come in through the courtyard. After everything had been arranged, Nanhe Khan messed it all up. He did not understand the subtlety of the arrangements. After leaving the courtyard he decided that it would be easier to exit by the front gate and take a rickshaw in the bazaar. Dada caught him, gave him a talking to, discharged him...

Mai's finalised, arranged plans were left unexecuted. Dada's one bark sent the artiste far from our house forever.

Then dada had the barbed wires at the back tightened up. He recited something to me in Sanskrit, the meaning of which was that women who sang or wore bells on their feet were bad women, and one whose teeth were a little protruding was a wise woman.

But dada was in favour of my learning English. It was dada who sent Subodh to a boarding school with some actual English teachers to turn him into an 'English' officer. The first time Subodh came home he had forgotten Hindi somewhat. When we were served okra at lunch, he could not remember that it was called bhindi. 'Give me that...that...that...' he pointed, dumb. Mai laughed.

Dada sent me too to the mission school in town which, in our nice, hot country, was misnamed 'Sunny Side Convent'. Dada wanted that I should learn English.

But not speak it. Or Hindi either. That is, not speak at all.

Even when dadi broke her leg, dada did not come to see her. He would call us to get the news and ask babu about everything. It was we who told him that dadi was all right after her operation, had been unconscious but was now awake. Now and then dada's lip could be seen trembling behind his moustache.

We were afraid of dada in our childhood. Even later we would try to avoid him. When Subodh came back from the hostel, he had long, puffed-up hair like a hero. He must have been fourteen or fifteen. Dada frowned, 'What is this?' His barber was summoned. 'He looks just like a Christian.' Subodh was strapped to a chair on the outside verandah, covered with a sheet and his head started on. Subodh's face was red with anger and tears, tense with embarrassment.

I went and told mai. Without saying anything, she washed her hands of flour, wiped them on her sari, covered her head, and advancing to the curtain, called out, 'Subodh, come here.'

Dada was in his sitting room. Mai came in, said clearly, 'That's enough. Yes, that's enough. Stop. Go inside.' And pulling aside Subodh's sheet, took him inside.

The haircut was already done, but dada had given orders for a total shave and Subodh was rescued just in time.

Subodh was two years younger than me. Dark, good looking, with long bones. We played together a lot. In the beginning I was advised—'Look after your younger brother.' After some time he was advised—'Look after your sister.'

When Subodh was born, dadi told us, babu had wept. Holding me tight in his lap he said—'I knew it, I knew it...Baba appeared to me in my dream...assured me it would be a boy.' Dada was also pleased. He named the baby Subodh; babu I think wanted to call him Kaustubh.

Dadi would put Subodh on her legs, her sari pulled up. She massaged him with mustard cooked in milk and dried, ground with sesame and poppyseed. The smell of it wafts to me from a distant childhood and settled down inside me. She would massage this mixture in, clean the dirt, then clothe him in a light shirt and leave him in the verandah with his noises—'Sunaina, keep an eye on your brother.'

Dadi had another pastime too. Until he was quite old she would massage Subodh and tickle him between the legs. 'Oh, my little one, my sweet one, my child...don't be naughty...don't wet your dadi with your Ganga water...'

She put Subodh to sleep with those same caresses and murmurings—'See how he is lying like a nawab, already a man... hee hee hee...his father was the same.'

Mai said that it was dadi who brought up Subodh, her own job was just to nurse him. Subodh had become an addict to nursing.

Even after he began to walk he ran for her breasts as soon as he saw mai. If mai ever stopped him, dadi was angry—'Oh dear, oh dear, is this all that's left for me to see? The mother cares for herself more than her son?'

Mai would bite her lips with pain—'Ammaji he bites, he should leave this habit now...' And dadi was furious—'Oh Ram, oh Ram, the child's health will be ruined, much she cares.' And then she even managed to shed a few tears.

It had reached the point that if Subodh cried for some reason and could not be silenced, dada, dadi, babu, each in his own way, would pronounce the same order—'Call mai, what's the matter, why is the child crying so much?' Mai would be red with shame and pull Subodh to her breast. Whatever time of the day or night.

Once mai had shown me her red, wounded breasts from Subodh's constant suckling.

She even gave them to me once saying, 'See, is there anything to have or does this boy keep suckling for nothing?' I don't remember if it was sweet or bitter. The breast was very soft and I took mai's milk very, very carefully.

I used to try to distract Subodh with something as soon as he cried, before the house could resound with summons for mai. If he was looking at mai and there was desire coming to light in his eyes, I would beat him to it by thrusting a biscuit or something into his mouth.

But Subodh and I got along well together. We would spend the whole day in the fields, on the trees, under the trees, on the roof, playing, eating, talking, wandering around. If nothing else, we kept snacking on jaggery, sugar crystals, sweetened roasted wheat powder. You put the powder in your mouth and did 'pooh—pooh'—and there was a dustcloud! We would be weak with laughter. At the first rain, we would run to get drenched, laughing at the battery of rock-like drops, jump with vexation at the itch in our palms, float paper boats in the drains, and hold our breaths and stand under the waterfall from the drainpipes on the roof. We splashed in the water, letting out fountains of laughter.

All my childhood the two of us were 'we'. After being 'we' for so long it wasn't easy to become separate.

But the 'after' itself wasn't easy.

Subodh slept between mai and me. At night it was I who got up to cover him. If he needed to go to the bathroom he woke me. If he had fever I checked him in the dark again and again to see how hot he was.

When I started going to school and babu tried to speak to me in English, I would be too shy to reply.

'Come on, speak,' dadi pinched me, 'otherwise in today's times no one will marry you.'

The matter was forgotten. But Subodh had become thoughtful and said quite a while later—'Never mind, dadi, I will marry Suni.'

Subodh never left me. He left the house but not me. He had only one refrain, which was to get me out of there too. He talked to me, got me clothes and books, all so that I would be good enough to get out of there.

One refrain—'Get out.'

And both of us had one refrain in common, that we would get mai out of there. I don't know when we had decided that mai's life, especially her future, was our business. Babu was not part of it, or maybe tangentially, through some connection to mai. The real ones were we three—mai, Subodh and I—whose actual lives were outside the house. Who were only passing time in the house.

There were those special evenings in one room, with mai, Subodh, and I. Then mai would tell us stories and we argued, quarrelled, talked. No one else entered that room, and the duties were not pre-allotted. Anyone could bring the water, anyone put up the mosquito nets, anyone bolt the doors, and anyone arrange the books.

Subodh and I had our own games. Toys had not overtaken the market yet. We did not have piles of toys; some for Subodh, some for me. Nor was it that there were guns and cars for him and dolls and kitchen sets for me. Yes, there were girls' toys and boys' toys, but they were not all completely coated with distinctions of gender.

Or was it we who washed the distinctions away? Babu brought clay fruits and vegetables and wooden kitchen utensils. Mai stuffed cotton and stitched wool and made cloth dolls. Bows and arrows came from the Dussehra mela, clay birds and animals from the Diwali market. Drums, flutes, kites, pots, a whole household came together!

If there was a shade of masculinity or femininity, it showed only accidently in passing.

We would play house together—make a clay oven, a real fire, and tea for Bhondu to drink. We played shop, and doctor-patient. I don't remember how the theatrics composed themselves, but we would move from one script to another, saying our dialogues. We even gave up language sometimes and would say sentences laden with emotion but made only of sounds and imitation words— *'Gaunchi paunchi, ay khe phu parandol kanmish byura!'*

We were, in turn, gardeners, cooks, grandchildren, neighbours. Our shop would be stocked with pebbles and twigs, leaves would act as money, the whole household could be created from clay. Any shortcoming was made up by fresh *harshringar* flowers, which we collected and threaded into garlands that were too small for the neck or the wrist, but could fill up the roles of many absent substances. Thus the doctor's medicines today, and the burglar's loot tomorrow. Everything in the house was like the joker in a pack of cards—funny and able to be made into anything we chose.

Our childhoods marched along together. Our schools were also the same till class four but from class five 'Sunny Side Convent' took only girls. Subodh was put into the boarding school in the big city, to learn English manners.

I was quite small then. I heard that Subodh was coming home. After a long time. I don't know why I suddenly felt shy. I ran and hid on the roof. I kept staring at the gate. Subodh came, taller, different, grown-up. In pants, tie, socks and shoes. The same face but changed. I felt a sudden question inside me—'How do I know that this is my brother?' But the strangeness vanished and it became normal for him to go and come. When he came it was as if we had always been together; when he left it was as if we had always been separate.

Subodh's prestige in our house increased hundredfold because of his leaving. Dada and babu practised their English on him at every chance. Mai did not know any English. Dadi could not even speak straight Hindi. The corners of our house echoed with many tongues.

Subodh would talk about his school. He swam, did horse riding, played football, hockey and cricket. He showed pictures of a dance at the annual function with a 'sister school'. He did ballroom dancing. He put his arm around my waist, took my hand in his other one, raised it, and danced to a tune on a record—'Like this.' In one picture there was a girl, covering her eyes and shouting. 'Don't!' Because she did not want to be recognised? In case her parents found out...?

His school had caning too. Subodh recounted with pride how if you made a mistake, you had to bend before everyone, lower your pants, and receive the cane. You got a blow if you uttered a Hindi word outside Hindi class. Subodh could speak English fluently. He even did 'Hi mom, bye mom,' and babu said, 'He speaks better than me. When the teacher himself is English...'

Subodh promised me, 'I will teach you good English, make sure you have a great accent, get you out of here...'

Even dadi was always eager to hear something from his fund of experiences. What happened at the station, how was it on the train, where did you go on the school trip, what were the programmes on Founder's Day, and so on.

Then it would be time for Subodh to go. He would tell mai that all the boys were crazy about her homemade *besan laddus* and to fill his tuck box with them.

The courtyard would be filled with the sweet smell of roasting gram flour in pure ghee, and the iron spatula in the iron wok would sound musically. Mai, wiping her hot face with the end of her sari, would bring the huge tray of besan to dadi, and dadi would press it with relish into balls, and give us some hot, fresh ones as well.

When Subodh went off to his boarding school I would be left alone. There were school friends, but I had contact with them only in school. The only ones who could be visited at home during Holi or Diwali were the few whose parents were known to babu or dada. Coincidentally these were the ones I was not too friendly with in school, that is, my *kachcha* friends. Then, if it turned out that one of them had a brother thirteen or fourteen years or older, dada would say clearly that all of us need not visit.

When I came home from school I would wander around the big compound of our house. In the guava orchard, or on the roof under the spreading mango limbs. Staring into the servants' quarters, or going out into the fields where the water was turned into the irrigation ditches by the buffaloes at the well. If dada saw me, he would stop me—'Go to mai.' Babu would also tell mai, 'Keep her near you. There's no trusting servants or anyone.' Dadi would say, 'The girl has come of age.' I would feel that a-girl-of-age was the name of a problem. With an odd sensation I looked inside myself for this problem. But given such a vast house and compound, who could stop me going anywhere, who could keep an eye on me?

Mai never stopped me from doing anything. I thought she paid no attention. But when she had to call me for a meal she sent Hardeyi straight to wherever I was—at the mud walls, inside the room, under the tree, or on the roof.

Nor did mai ever scold. There were things that made me tremble in anticipation. If I am caught, this is the end, and what the hell, I'll tell a lie. But mai simply did not ask and I did not have to tell a lie.

At one time I began to steal money. A man selling pink, orange, and multicoloured ice creams began coming to our school in the break. The tastiest and the most popular was the five-paisa incomparable mixture of frozen sugar and water. I would collect money on the sly. Bhondu returned change to Hardeyi, Hardeyi to mai, mai kept it here or there or gave it to me to put away, and I practised my sleight of hand. Then, once, I saw mai put away ten rupee notes in a trunk and I made three or four notes vanish from there.

Mai asked me, 'Do you know where the money is kept?'

Because mai never asked, as soon as she did, I lost my wits. I stammered—'Yes...yes...I think I saw it...in an envelope...between my books...'

And I took out the wretched envelope from my bag and handed it to mai.

The matter ended there.

Today I wonder how I thought at all that mai did not know. And if mai knew why did she not say anything?

Mai did not, as it were, know anything. She heard what you told her, never tried to find out any more. Once I found a book in babu's room with strange pictures. I hid and began to study them. Mai entered, and said with perfect calm, 'You are reading babu's book, is it interesting?' 'It's dirty, mai, look,' I passed the book to her, inspired by her calm, ordinary voice. 'Hmmm...h'm... yes, it's strange...such things are sold so quickly whether you learn anything from them or not.' Mai neither stayed around nor did she remove the book from there. I looked through it without hurrying, digested what mai had said without hurry. So there must be other books which do not sell so well, and if I take this as the truth, how will I ever learn?

Mai left us alone like this again and again. It was as if she did not know how to feel suspicious. 'Theft' was one thing, 'dirty book' was another thing, and we were yet a thing apart. Separate and good. Her faith in us made us believe in ourselves.

But this faith also made us afraid, bent under a heavy responsibility.

We used to think of mai as our burden. Since we became conscious, we were trying to lift her, balance her, save her. We grew up in the longing to save her. Her weight bent us. Others used her as an excuse to bend us. She was the hostage put in front while dada, dadi, babu—all aimed their wishes and orders at us.

We did not understand her profound faith in us to be the well of strength that it was. We just kept crying at her helplessness. Babu told her that she was a formless pot, a lota that would roll wherever it was pushed. He told her that the children made a fool of her. She would begin to tell us what he wanted, then start listening to our story instead, and keep quiet in such a way that we could go ahead and do whatever was on our minds even more brazenly.

Babu, of course, believed that he was never fooled by us, whether it was a matter of seeing a movie or a play, going to the friend's house who had a brother, or deciding to take Science, not Arts. Mai would see us off from the courtyard gate and keep up such an appearance that babu would keep believing that we were playing around somewhere, on the roof, eating guavas, sucking sugarcane. It was mai who signed my form for 'Biology'.

Later mai consented to be made an even greater fool of, to use what would be babu's language. She welcomed Subodh's foreigner fiancée and kept my live-in friend Vikram at home as if he was its natural legatee. Mai never called Subodh's Judith sinful like babu did because of her alcohol and cigarettes. There was something in her that refused to pass judgement. She permitted the other person to reveal himself layer by layer before her. When she liked something, she respected it. When she was touched, she gave her love unconditionally. In this gaze of mai's, we had to stop pretending.

It was this same faith that injected some solemnity into the middle of all my innocent fidgeting around.

Dadi's scolding could not do it. Dadi disliked my fidgeting around. Any kind of restlessness made her angry.

'Sit properly, what is this with your legs open like a bazaar woman?'

If I lay down flat on the bed dadi covered me with her sheet immediately—'Learn, you fool, that a man's eye is like an eagle's. Don't expose yourself like this.'

I mentioned 'love marriage' once and dadi was on fire—'Go ahead, send her to an English school.'

That's the way dadi was. Once the sweeper's wife was bitten by a snake. Someone came running, 'Bahuji, bahuji, Champi has been bitten by a snake.' Subodh was there. He leapt up and ran out. When I leapt up dadi scolded, 'Sit down quietly, you don't need to run around everywhere.'

I sat down ashamed, feeling that curiosity was somehow shameful.

Babu would tell mai, 'Keep an eye.' When Subodh was home, we would play carrom with babu's friend's son and daughter at the club. I was mad about winning. Once I was so near victory that even though I had to go to the bathroom, I could not bring myself to leave the game. A Newton-defying idea came to my head—why not just do it sitting here, only my panties will get wet after all! I did it. What I didn't think of—I am hoping I was really tiny at the time—was the sound which immediately alerted everyone. Subodh peeped underneath, 'Oh, Suni, you've done it.' He was two years younger than me. All I could do was insist, 'No, no, I haven't done anything.' But my insistence could not stop the sound that started. Some things once started cannot be stopped. Subodh was equally insistent, 'Yes, yes, look under your chair.' The son and daughter of the 'friend' were not looking underneath.

Yes, I must have been small. But even at that time babu would ask mai, why was I friendly with the son when the daughter was there as well?

Everyone was worried. Only mai did not seem to care, where I was, what I did. Everyone was anxious to put me behind the 'real parda', and she, as it were, accidentally pushed the curtain open before it could be stretched shut and closed tightly.

She was in a minority, however, that pushed the parda open whenever she could. The majority held it tight with such determination that the parda would not really open. I was a little inside, a little outside, when maybe I did begin to do the real parda. The eyes became downcast, voice low, shoulders somewhat hunched...

But there was an ember glowing behind the parda that caught the wind, and flared up from the repeated shaking of the parda, bursting into flame and setting fire to the parda itself.

Dadi would say that mai lit this fire. Dada would say that it was Subodh's doing. Babu would keep rubbing his chest so that he would not have a heart attack.

And mai?

She would not say anything. She herself knew about pardas. When her parda was threatened by a fire she must have drawn the flame inside rather than let it grow outwards.

This was yet another difference between mai and me. Her flame went inwards, mine outwards. But there was a fire that burned in each case...

But fire has no part in my childhood. And apparently no part in mai's tale at all. Her fire was never seen in childhood, or youth, or old age. She must have pulled her flame in and hidden it so well that the coolness which emanated had no trace of sparks in it at all. We could only suspect her fire. Only guess at it.

And do as much only when we got around not to thinking, but reflecting on our thoughts. When it became impossible for contradictory ideas to live peacefully together. When the voiceless shadow caught in the net of oppressors forced us to reflect on the meaning of 'voiceless'. We had seen ourselves fighting everyone, keeping her safe behind us. That we stayed safe behind her was a thought we never permitted ourselves to think. Or having thought it, did not admit the thought.

We did not acknowledge a mai outside us. Her life had begun, after all, with our births.

It was only later that the cool remains of her fire were there to see. And by then layers of those ashes could be found on so many things.

We had known only that we were in mai and mai was made for us. That is why we could go mad with anger seeing her act like everyone's puppet, and having to live on their leftovers. If dada wanted some delicacy he got it, when no one wanted it, mai got it. Dadi was fond of a certain exquisite savoury so it was hers, when it became stale it was mai's. Whatever babu left over was mai's. Whatever we liked was what mai quietly decided she did not like.

Dada and dadi could not stand food from the fridge—dadi said that refrigerated food became 'bad'—meaning both stale and 'evil'. So that was all for mai. If by some chance the dish cooked in the morning appeared at night then dadi would start off—'You do what you have to do, but for us old people make two fresh rotis if possible. Otherwise tell me, and I will manage it myself. Thanks to the lord my hands and feet are not completely gone yet. They still move.'

We became more alert after a while. We began to scold mai for her habits. 'You have no wishes of your own...you are passive,' we would scold her. We ended the system where hers was the last turn and she got the leftovers. Dadi was abusive: 'Mai is acting simple to lord it over others.' But our only care was to fill mai with thoughts of independence.

Once we tricked her. We bought fruit. It was winter and there were apples, peaches, apricots in plenty. Lovely red, ripe peaches. I bit into one—'No taste in these peaches.' Subodh tasted one— 'They are crumbly inside. I'll eat only apples.'

And we saw that for two days mai did not touch any other fruits but ate only the peaches!

We gave her hell and forced her to eat the other fruit.

It seemed that it was our task to not leave mai empty but fill her up with everything. Who else did she have but us?

Once we had some guests who we heard were mai's distant relatives. We paid no attention to this matter.

The guests stayed two days. As soon as they left, the house resounded with dada's booms. When they had arrived they had touched dada's feet and he had asked, 'Who are you?' When they left dada was reading his newspaper in his sitting room. They touched his feet but dada did not notice and kept reading his paper as before.

As soon as they were gone the newspaper was finished. 'How did these people arrive here? It's amazing, I must say, after hearing such frank things about themselves, they could still hold their heads high and come.'

Dada would begin again louder upon seeing babu, 'Can you believe their shamelessness? Here I was, quiet out of civility, but it will surely be considered my cowardice?'

Then, as if by the way, he said, 'Did bahu happen to write any letters home? Find out. After all, how did they dare come here? She used to write quietly before as well, even meet them secretly. I don't want to say it but those people...and the priest and his great son...'

When babu came in to dadi, mai said, a little louder than usual, 'Please tell father-in-law that I had no idea Bitten would come. I myself do not want anyone to come and be insulted.'

Babu showed anger in a weak, whining voice, 'Why would we want to show disrespect to anyone? Are we doing that? That son of your priest...'

Mai said, 'Why is it necessary to bring him into it?'

Then dadi displayed fire with her eyes, 'Well, if your heart is as pure as Ganga water then why are you getting so worked up? First you make a mistake, then you try to boss around your seniors.'

Mai lowered her head.

We were small. But a desire to protect mai came forth. 'Don't say anything to mai.'

Today that voice of mai's seems full of pride, full of dignity. And dadi's? That was a voice defeated. Alone. Tired.

We kept trying to save mai. She is weak, a puppet, she has no one but us. So weak that when we do battle for her she retreats at the very moment of climax and our war cry shatters uselessly to pieces in all directions. For instance, Subodh bought tickets for a play. Mai got ready in a silk sari. Babu commented as he came out, 'You are going too? Are you sure?' And mai stopped. Subodh kept ranting, but mai changed her sari and went into the kitchen.

This is clear enough. This we saw clearly even then. But there was much we did not see clearly. Once dada lifted his hand to strike Subodh, who was insisting that I should go to the hostel. Mai entered the sitting room, and met dada's gaze for perhaps the only time in her life. Dada's hand dropped, mai pulled Subodh inside, and he eventually dropped me off to the hostel.

Then we saw a blue bruise on her arm. We did not know what had happened but we were running in the fields high with wheat, and babu was in the club with that woman and we didn't know who else. 'Babu, mai is going away.' Babu came back. Mai took off her watch and hit babu with it, 'Go and give this to her also.' We slept holding her hand that night. Sometimes we asked, 'Mai, where were you going?' 'Nowhere,' she said, 'I wouldn't leave you and go anywhere.'

Naturally. Because there could be no mai away from us.

To get something by sacrificing something is an old tradition of ours. When mai offered a sacrifice, others got the fruit. There was a long list of fasts that she kept. Ahoyi, Teej, Lalhichhat, Thursday, Monday, Shivratri, Ganeshchaturthi, Jyutiya. Some for the husband's prosperity, some for the son's health, some for her children.

Nine days after Dussehra mai kept the Karva Chauth fast for her husband's long life and happiness. She did not drink water the whole day. In the evening she exchanged a *karva*, a clay pot with a spout, with dadi or bua. She kept it in the puja with some sprouts inside. Wearing her bridal clothes, she did puja and sent the Brahman some gifts and food. Then she read the story of the fast which we would arrive to hear with interest. There was a lovely sister with seven brothers who could not bear to see her go hungry and thirsty. So they climbed a tree and lit a lamp behind the leaves, saying, look, sister, the moon is out, break your fast. And she did so and news came that her husband had died. Then she did penance; the devi appeared and told her the way. For a whole year the sister prayed near her dead husband and kept the Karva Chauth fast. The husband arose.

That was the story. After reading it mai searched for the moon, we tripping alongside, but we couldn't show her a false moon after hearing the story, could we? The slim moon of the fourth night, like a shard of a glass bangle. That night it would not appear before eight or nine. When she saw it mai worshipped it, offered water from her pot, turned around seven times, did *aarti*, then came and ate her puris and vegetables, which she had cooked herself.

Teej was also kept by mai for babu. Teej came in the light fortnight of Bhadon. Again a fast without water. She got Ganga mud and made Shiva and Parvati, decorated her puja place with banana leaves, and offered fruit, sweets, puris, *sindur, bindi,* bangles, mirror, comb, *alta,* sari, etc., which she sent to bua after her puja. The next morning she would bathe, do puja, and put sindur in her parting from Parvati's sindur. The images and flowers all went to the Ganga for immersion. After feeding and gifting the Brahman, she finally broke her fast around ten with a sweet.

And then she kept Mondays, Thursdays, and god knows what other fasts. These days of fasts and feasts were special playdays for us for a long time. They meant sitting near a beautiful, dressed-up mai in an incense-filled puja room and eating delicious things. Later, we could not recollect any fast that was for the health or happiness of the wife. Not that I know any even now.

However, there was a fast that babu kept. Navratra, the Nine Nights of the Goddess. He kept a fast every day of the nine and broke it on the ninth day. He did not speak till his bath in the morning. He clapped to call the servant, or mai, or me. Then he told us with gestures whatever he wanted—the newspapers, his bath water, his shaving things. Mai would say in advance—'Take this, go and give it, there will be a clap for it just now'—and there would be a clap. When we showed surprise she said, 'This is my job. What use is my work if after all these years together I cannot tell what he wants?'

Babu did not eat the whole day. Nor did he drink water. There is great strength in devotion, and babu kept a fast as if it was no trouble at all, he did not feel any hunger or thirst or tiredness. The same work, meditation, routine. His face was not any paler, his walk no less steady.

In the evening before sunset, mai would take a bath, wash the kitchen, and go barefoot into it to cook food. During that time we were all forbidden to enter the kitchen. Mai made special pure, *satvik* food. *Rotis* out of water-chestnut flour. A potato dish with rock salt. Some green vegetable. *Raita* with yogurt. And *halwa, kheer,* or *rabri,* some sweet decorated with nuts and raisins and spices.

As it grew dark babu would appear from somewhere. He took a bath, wore saffron, and sat at his puja. His sacred thread shone on his bare chest. The lamp was lit, the recitation was made, and the incense smoke curled into the courtyard, signalling mai. She would arise, serve the food in bowls on the thali and deliver it to the puja room. It was duly offered, the aarti was taken, and leaving the food babu would go and sit in his room. There his voice would call out—'Let's have it.' Mai would put the tray of of food in front of him and keep refilling whichever bowl became empty.

Then it was our turn to tuck in.

The greatest fun was at the end of the whole Navratra. On the ninth day there was a special puja and it was a day of glory for me. Once in a while babu went off to Kashi or Vindyachal to do this last puja. But if he was at home then either seven or nine girls were respectfully fed in our house. I was included in those girls. Subodh had no takers that day, no matter what dadi may have liked.

Mai seated us in a row. Brahman girls were called from around about and, in turn, our feet were washed and we were served halwa, puri, vegetables and chickpeas on large leaf plates. But the real, wonderful 'item' was after dinner when mai would anoint our foreheads one by one and touch our feet. That's right, mai would bend and touch our feet and fold her hands! Then she would give us some money.

This business of touching the feet would strike me as exceedingly funny. I would feel shy, giggle, go into fits of laughter. As if it were play acting. Mai would touch my feet and I would burst out laughing.

One time bua had come at Navratra. And when the girls were lined up, there was suddenly a cry that one was missing. Mai sent Bhondu off on his cycle to go and fetch someone.

Subodh and I were counting and there seemed the right number. How could these grown-ups make such a mistake? There are enough of us, mai, look, one, two, three...I counted nine.

'Oh, you idiot,' bua laughed, 'You're counting yourself? You are no longer auspicious! You cannot be counted among the goddesses, you lucky one.'

Dadi began croaking with laughter from her seat—'Come here, my dear old woman, where do you want to go so pure and holy?'

Everyone was laughing.

I understood and did not understand at the same time. I felt myself grow hot inside. I could not raise my eyes to meet anyone's.

Then mai said to bua—'What are you doing, bibiji, let the child remain a child.' She pushed me gently saying—'You are the first of the auspicious girls. Of course you will eat. Come on, hold out your feet for me...'

Mai could not save me from falling into the pit, but she put down a ladder immediately for me.

Childhood was departing but mai forcefully stopped it and handed it back to me.

I had gone and scolded Hardeyi, 'Look at your ironing, you've burnt my frock, look.' Hardeyi took it to mai and mai explained that now I could also be a mother.

Why then was it so impure to be able to become a mother? Mai rescued me from this shame.

Mai never told me that on certain days I should not go into the puja, or into the kitchen, or not eat in the usual place.

That was what my childhood was like. Falling into the pit again and again and climbing up by a ladder. Girls' childhoods can go very suddenly, and mine went too, only not so suddenly or so easily.

There was a ladder on which I could climb back up. So the ladder has great significance in my childhood.

The ladder and the pit.

Mai could not stop me from falling into the pit, because there were so many people around who were eager to push me in. But she would come from behind and quickly put down a ladder for me to limp back up.

Our childhood moulders and guardians were these: our grandfather, dada, who used to be a landlord, and whose feet babu would touch, for form's sake, and after saying his 'charanasparsh, babuji' would then carefully avoid; our grandmother, dadi, who was our mother's mother-in-law and had been her own mother-in-law's daughter-in-law; our father, babu, who was a raja and beloved by his mother more than he could ever hope to be by a lover; our mother, mai, who was uneducated, voiceless, and a round pot without shape—all because she made up her mind on the basis of the scene unfolding before her, rather than on preconceptions.

The deepest etched image of this childhood remains our togetherness, saving mai, getting out the house, and getting mai out. Mai was with us when we fed the peacocks in the courtyard. We asked mai for the chaff from the flour to dust on to the anthills and then watched their teeming activity. We gave fitting responses to those who attacked mai with insults and sarcasm. We left the house by the back door known only to mai, to my girlfriends who had brothers and to other odd, exciting places. We lived together in one room and shared everything.

But our school did not take boys after class four and Subodh went off to another city, and I went alone every morning on a red rickshaw to 'Sunny Side Convent'. We had nuns in our school who were either from South India or, red-faced, from Ireland. Mother Maria played the piano while we sang Christmas carols:

—Silent night, holy night
All is calm, all is bright...

and

—The first Noel
The angels did sing...

The first period in school was Moral Science, every day. We did an exam on it but the marks were not counted in the finals. We were taught morality preached by Jesus Christ and other great Western religious figures, after which we were considered fortified with good thoughts for good conduct for the whole day.

Sometimes the padre came to speak to us. The whole school gathered in the hall and we rejoiced that two or three periods would be wasted that way.

Father told us, 'Dear girls, the Lord has made you perfect like apples, round, red, sweet. But, remember, to keep this you must not let anyone touch you. Bite an apple and you mar its beauty.'

We were things to look at.

It seems that no one had told him that an apple was not something to look at, but to taste. It's sweet. If you just keep it, it will dry and rot and worms will finish it up inside.

That is, if we chose to be precise about his suggestion of apples, we were things to taste.

Thus, we were taught from childhood about being apples. You are an apple, be careful, very careful, look out, save yourself, look out for the tasters, save yourself.

The fact that one day the apple would be tasted was an unspoken truth on which hung a huge lock of silence.

The school had a library that had only English books. First we had Enid Blyton, then romances. The nun in charge of the library took great interest in recommending books. 'This one, a beautiful romance by Barbara Cartland...ohhhh...' The heroine of these stories was a seventeen- or eighteen-year-old novice who had just graduated from some convent like ours and was taking her first trembling steps in the wide world. The hero would be quite a bit older than her, rich, a count or earl or baron or duke. An experienced flirt. A sceptic who had experienced life's bitterness. He had known treacherous women, hypocrisy and lies, selfishness and injustice, and all the illusions of this world. Now he had become hard, a rough Casanova who sought only pleasure, who believed in no one, who had only bitter smiles and sour remarks for everyone around him. He played free with innumerable beauties. He wandered around with utter abandon everywhere. And then enters—TA DA—the childlike, innocent, tender-as-a-petal, ignorant-about-the-world, simple, truthful, somewhat stupid, lovely heroine who collapses before the harsh attacks of the hero, shrinks, sheds tears. And then he takes her in his arms and keeps kissing her for three or four pages. In the hero's clasp the heroine becomes aware of her soft body next to his iron masculinity, and she is leaning on him, swooning, her head is swimming as if drunk and she becomes limp like a vine next to a tree... But it is the hero who falls down and picking up the hem of her skirt kisses it and says in a husky voice—I love you, only you, you have returned hope to my life, can you accept this sinner? And the heroine's voice trembles with excitement, oh I love you, she whispers in a kind of daze and both lose themselves in a great spiritual love.

This was the literature that we and also our nuns read in school.

In Subodh's library, however, there were the English classics— Dickens, the Brontë sisters, Hardy and George Eliot. He began to give me these books to read. On reading them I built up pictures in my imagination which came to life years later when I first set foot in England. It was as if my eyes were opened, my breath raced with pleasure, my heart beat in excitement—why, this is the 'heath' and 'meadow' and 'heather' and 'bracken' and 'ivy' and 'daffodil' that I've known from my childhood. All the pictures came to life.

I had felt love for the lotus blooming in the pond and the melon and cucumber vines on the sand as well, but there was romance in it. With England there was this ancient, spiritual relationship. I had imbibed its romance as a concentrated elixir, as it were, in my childhood.

Now I wonder what I really was familiar with—the health and meadow or the lotus and melon? Or with any of them? But then I was only aware how intimate everything located on English soil seemed to be. And all this experience was brought to me by Subodh.

When Subodh came home mai would say happily—'Tell your sister everything also, she should also know everything.'

Subodh knew a lot. Even dada's guests would call out for Subodh. He could argue with all of them. About Western culture, the ways of a big city, politics, history, all kinds of things.

Babu, too, was impressed, especially with Subodh's knowledge of English. 'Make her English good also.' He wanted that I too should speak at breakneck speed. If I spoke at all. Subodh also took a fancy to being my teacher.

It's true that I had reached a point where I would have won a competition for mixed speech. I could not speak a sentence without jumbling up languages. The languages were one of the 'heath', the other of the 'melon', English and Hindi. A whole sentence could be in English but at least one word would have to be in Hindi—'I was saying *ki...*'

And if I was speaking in Hindi, the same thing—'*Wah* before *a gayi thi to main tayar...*'

Subodh became critical of this eloquent technique.

There was a remarkable phase when, whether I could speak Hindi or not, he wanted me to speak English. The world has moved ahead rapidly outside this house, he told me. Move with it. Master it.

We sat down to eat and I had only to open my mouth, 'Pass the *dal*,' that he would correct me, 'In what language madam?'

I often repeated myself in English but also often kept silent in stubbornness.

He complained to mai, 'You ask me to teach her but...' And mai would persuade me, 'Speak a little, he is only doing it for your own good.' And I would be angry that everyone could forget, including me, that I was the older by two years. Who was Subodh to teach me anyway?

Subodh had left for the big city, Englishmen were his teachers, he had seen thousands of things, he had experienced foreign things like dance parties. He had shown me pictures from these parties. Apart from me he had shown only mai. His prestige kept increasing in our house, well beyond the artificial barriers of age. He could speak with dada and babu as an equal.

Everyone had high hopes of him and lots of confidence in him. Something in Subodh helped him not to bend down under the weight of all this hope and confidence but let him develop the same hope and faith and take wing with them, higher, higher, forward, beautifully. He was at the top of his class in his studies every year, he won prizes in sports, and then one day he got a national scholarship to study in England.

We were all aware that Subodh had been dreaming of studying in England from the time he topped in school. He went back to college early one vacation to get his proposal ready in consultation with his teachers. At home, too, he would listen for hours to dada reminiscing about the freedom struggle and take notes in his diary.

He went to one place for an examination, to another for an interview. Babu had a special puja performed for his success. In the days that followed he waited impatiently for the results. I decided not to eat anything each morning till the arrival of the postman.

This was how I happened to keep a 'fast'. I was getting impatient just like Subodh, and only one thought filled my mind, 'Let him get it, dear god, let him get it!' Just as I was about to put a bite into my mouth one morning, my mind on this prayer, I stopped. I thought that if I could 'bear' to not eat, he would 'get' it. The 'fast' started just like that. To mai's insistence that an empty stomach all morning was not a good thing, I pleaded that I was dieting, I was unable to digest what I was eating, and that I would just have lunch. The 'fast' was kept until the news came in the post.

Once, earlier on, babu had said something to mai. We could not hear what, mai did not show anything, and the daily routine was the same, but somewhere we understood and were worried.

At night we could hear mai's voice in babu's room, and it seemed disturbed, pained. We woke each other up, and I, then Subodh, called out to mai—'We can't sleep, mai.' Babu told us to go to sleep, mai would come shortly after pressing his head. But

we really could not sleep. We kept calling, and did not give up till
we had saved mai.

One night somewhere around that time we opened our eyes
and saw mai at our desk writing something in the light of the
lamp. We nudged each other and kept watching her silently. She'll
commit suicide...she's planning to run away...that was the kind of
thing we were thinking. Then we began to call out to her.

And then one day after mai had done puja and lit the little lamp,
my foolish brain said, 'Sacrifice.' Stand on one leg while the lamp
burns, until the wick goes out, 'bear it', and everything will be all
right for mai. I stood on one leg. People would get suspicious if I
stayed in the puja room, so I began to hop around from one room
to another. I would peep in to see if the wick was still burning, if
my 'sacrifice' time was over or not.

I did not tell even Subodh. He laughed in ignorance. 'What
are you doing, Suni?' I said, 'I'm trying to see how long I can
last on one leg.' He was not interested, his mind must have been
elsewhere, and he turned away. He was younger than me, after all,
and naturally a little sillier too.

I was at my 'sacrifice' for a few minutes, but it seemed like
hours. Fed up, I pulled the wick into the oil and put it out. That
made me restless and I lit the lamp again. Somehow it was finally
time to put both legs down. In passing I saw babu put his arm
around mai as she bent to give him something—and I took it to be
the effect of my 'sacrifice'.

There was an effect. On me. Of mai. Of generations of mais
who had done penance for others, made them successful, and
considered that their own success. Their breaths had filled the very
air from which I drew my own breath. I could try to push them
out of me but they came in again with every breath I took.

Mai, who was always giving, was a part of me. But had I not
been fighting for my right to take, and not to give?

I cannot become another mai. Mai herself is a vanishing
species. Even if I could become another mai I would not like to be

one. I will not be one. I will fight to the death not to be another mai. I want to pull out of myself every bit of mai. I want to drag out and throw away any tendency to 'sacrifice'. A foolish, wrong tendency, which I must defeat.

And yet it is mai, who is not my goal, who is everything I must fight, who is precisely that which I must not become—it is this mai before whom I repeatedly bow my head.

In my eagerness I fluttered my wings. Must not be mai, must not be a prisoner, must not stay bent over.

Mai had shown me a bird in the sky who was trying so hard to fly in one place. 'Look,' in that infinity of a sky the bird was flapping its wings without going anywhere. The whole sky was the bird's. But what use was it? What use was an empty endless sky?

I am forced to pay respect to this tireless, weak person who gave protection to the strong me. She was the one who undid my chains, let the fire inside me grow, and gave me strength. It was her tireless weakness that enabled me to fight.

I did not know that a pointless fluttering strength in a vast limitless sky was useless, but that a weakness that spread equally limitlessly could turn into strength.

It was when I emerged into the open air only to snatch my breath in the blows of the free wind that I realised how suffocating freedom could be.

But that also came later.

What came before were my own 'fasts' that made babu love mai again and brought Subodh his announcement of success by post. That self-denial is a source of power, that sacrifice is a means of achieving the desired goal, these and other such beliefs came and lodged within me in countless silent ways.

Subodh reached England. A line now joined our house to England. The hope of getting out and taking others out now began to swing boldly on that line.

There were many fights regarding this getting out. Remember that fights are not necessarily about fisticuffs.

By the time I was in the ninth or tenth class, Subodh and I both held firm that I would also go to a good school in a good place. Dada and dadi decided 'no', babu was shocked, and mai asked, 'What is the need, what do you lack here?'

'Then why did you send Subodh?' Her not being on my side made me feel weak at the knees.

'I would never have sent him. This was your babu and dada's decision. A school, no matter how great, cannot be like a home. The food and everything else...look, you can count his bones.'

When mai was not with me, I was helpless.

Subodh got the forms by post. An excellent school, in the mountains, run by nuns. 'Mai, just sign. Let her get admitted, then we can decide whether she will go or not.'

Mai looked at us sorrowfully and bent down and signed.

Dada and dadi brought the house down. 'Is this what will go on here?' Babu kept lecturing mai, 'Watch the children, forbid them.' Subodh would say angry things. Mai would be silent. And I was suspended halfway up the ladder, neither falling into the pit, nor standing safely on top.

Babu organised a katha in the name of Turiyatit baba for auspicious lives for all of us. A space was cleared in the courtyard with mud and cowdung. A pedestal of flour was made with a brass pot of water in the middle, mango stems foreclosed it, a bowl of rice was placed on it, and at the very top a clay lamp. Mai made a *panjiri* with flour, sugar and five dried fruits. She made *charanamrit* with fresh milk, yogurt, sugar, basil, the five dried fruits, honey and Ganga water. The sacrificial fire was lit. The panditji made us offer money for this and that, we all faced east and heard the recitation, so that Truth and Rightfulness be protected.

They were!

I did not manage to go—the letter was received after the interview date. The moment of conflict was averted. Amen!

I'd be damned if I ever sat in such a ritual again...

This is also how superstitions work!

Dadi may have loved us with her heart but our recent contrariness had begun to bother her. Subodh's readiness to talk back, my fidgeting all the time and dreaming of getting out. She started to accuse mai of secretly inciting us and even scolded Subodh for answering back to dada.

Subodh had said to dada that people like him, who were always preaching to 'Stay inside, let outsiders know nothing about you,' were actually the very ones who were always trying to see inside others' front doors.

Dada in fact took particular interest and pleasure in others' affairs. He had a voice that announced it to all of us. Affairs such as which problems were taking my girlfriend's father to court, or the reputed wayward ways of one of Subodh's teachers, and other such trivia.

If babu was present, mention would also be made of mai and 'the priest's son'. The mention would be veiled but the voice so full of secrets that we would lift our heads and look at mai.

Dada also had his own pronouncements about people's caste and kin. 'This is his way. Well, what's the wonder, he is a Kayasth after all.' 'That is his way. Well, that is the Punjabi style.' Even when he praised he did not leave out the caste and sect. 'So he may be a Muslim but he is very loyal.' Or, 'Can you believe that he is a baniya? You'll never find another like him in his caste.'

He had many jokes about names as well. 'A Gupta is a *kutta* (dog). A Srivastava is indeed (*vastava*) a *siri* (a Muslim lineage).

A Khanna is *pakhanna* (shit). A Saksena is a *sena* (army) of *shak* (suspicion). A Pandit—the p stands for *pakhandi* (hypocrite), the rest for *adambar* (luxury).' In this wave of nasty punning, the priest with the 'questionable character' and his son would again be dragged in.

At one time we made the mistake of asking dadi how *she* did not happen to be at the nexus of pujas and fasts.

'My dear, what do I need all that for? When my god is right in front of me why do I need stone gods? It is my good fate that I am able to keep serving my god.'

Then, targetting mai, she said—'From *some* kind of serving even god may turn his face.'

Her head swaying, eyes wide in their sockets, she told me— 'There must be some defect in me if my lord turns away from me and lets himself be worshipped by someone else.'

We had also seen the cardigan knitted by mai...

I must say we never saw babu actually treat mai roughly. He said very little to mai at all. Even his forbidding her to go out with us was done with two words rather than any clear direction. How can one blame him at all, in fact, when it was mai who herself shifted back as soon as he raised his eyes and looked at her? For his own jobs, such as having a button stitched, a tear mended, he would merely say, 'It's broken,' or, 'It's torn.'

Babu never interfered in the housework. He was hardly ever at home. He could be seen briefly when he came in to talk to dadi, otherwise we would have no idea where he was. He did not even have a personality like dada's that could always announce whether he was in or out. At mealtimes mai would say, 'Go and see if babu is here,' and we would go and see. Sometimes babu returned late at night and mai got up to heat his food. Sometimes babu would say he had already eaten.

No, we had never seen babu scream, hit, or threaten. He kept very busy. When mai began to have backaches and was forced to rest for a few minutes now and then to straighten her back, he would ask, 'What is it?' and leave without waiting for an answer. Maybe he could not imagine that there was actually anything. An illness could be appreciated if the body broke out, as in leprosy, or spilled out, with some kind of a pus. Mai's illness was such that neither did she have fever, nor even a cold or sinus. There was only a kind of momentary snapping inside her that is difficult to name or categorise.

Or an illness could be like dadi's, which made her scream and thrash her limbs in pain until babu massaged her.

Later—it is impossible to resolve this 'later' and 'earlier' conundrum—mai's back was always bent. That was old age though, which is itself an illness.

Babu began to gather new conveniences for mai. Even dada and dadi became addicted to ice from the fridge. And yet it seemed that mai enjoyed only those jobs in which she had to bend over. When the day's tea and meals, snacks and drinks, were done with, there would be *papads* to be rolled, *baris* to be dried, pickles to be made and spices to be ground. The paste of local rose petals was being made, or else the marmalade of *anvlas*. Thanks to the ladies' cooking sessions at the club, jams, jellies, sauces were also being cooked and carefully sealed in bottles. One could well ask: food, food, and more food, was there nothing else in life?

We asked. Mai got irritated. 'Why don't you understand? I enjoy this. These things are for everyone. If I don't do all these jobs in the house, what would I do? Go to school or college instead?'

If mai did not do 'this', she would sit in the courtyard and wrap wool, then wash it out, then knit. And all through, be bent over.

Dadi could not stand this concern of ours. She may have felt that she was the old one, the lovely one, the poor one, and instead we had eyes only for mai and were always trying to talk to her.

Dadi must have become even harsher. I had insisted that I would study Biology and be a doctor, and mai had signed the forms. I had passed High School with Science.

Dadi would pronounce: 'Here she goes to become a doctor on the strength of 55 marks. Everyone says that in this subject you can get 100 out of 100, but who will listen to me? I am an old hag after all. When the mother herself is bent on pushing the girl into the well...'

She kept muttering: 'I also happen to know about women doctors. They can't get married, and what do they get instead? Don't ask me to open my mouth before this girl. The mother is determined to have the daughter follow in her footsteps. Taking the advice of that priest all right. Oh, god, remove me from this place...'

We had an aunt, our bua, whom I had never forgiven for that Navaratra feast. She always echoed dadi's opinions. Once we happened to list the names of great women—Madame Curie, Sarojini Naidu, Virginia Woolf—and she laughed, 'Yes, yes, certainly, we will be proud that our girl has become so famous, but is wandering around in the garden the whole day the recipe for becoming a Madame Curie?'

Bua also never tired of saying that someone who wanted to be great could become so even in the middle of the kitchen, the stove, and the flour. It was only an excuse that I could not get ahead because of these.

Subodh once recounted how the fat Ganpat Rai had been welcomed by a crowd, and I happened to ask, 'Who is he?'

'God, Suni, you don't know the name of our Chief Minister?'

Dadi laughed unpleasantly, 'Do people become doctors knowing all this?'

Then bua spoke up. 'Is it only you who wants to be something? I too wanted to study a lot. All my studies were turned to ashes in the stove. Which woman escapes the kitchen and stove?'

I did not ask about the boast that someone who wanted to be something could be so anywhere. I remember keeping quiet with shame. Frustration with the kitchen stove and the ignorance of not knowing the Chief Minister of our state were two faces of the same coin. It was after that that dada's new complaint could be heard. 'So. Who has taken away the newspaper?'

Bua was not bad at heart. She was also very fond of us. She embroidered saris for me, stitched kurta-pyjamas for Subodh. She made us coriander punches when she came. They were lovely.

Babu and mai would stay up late when she came. Babu would take everyone out in rickshaws, to the market, the temples, the river, the club. Bua was jolly and laughed loudly at everything. Even at some odd idea of mine that dadi made fun of.

Phupha was half-dead in front of bua, in body as well as mind. Bua would tell all the stories, interrupting phupha, and then blame him. Poor phupha tried again and again to formulate a sentence but bua would continue it for him and complete the story. His voice would join her statements here and there like commas and fullstops. When he did manage to say something, bua turned the thing around in the middle and criticised him as well.

As for instance when phupha was telling us about someone and bua took on—'Ask me about him. Not a hint of his sorrow can be seen on his face. And what sorrow! One son is in jail, another in the other world, the wife has walked out. But a smiling face that always makes you smile. Always soft spoken. Sad in another's pain, happy in another's pleasure. When his mother was alive at least he had someone, though she was just a bundle on a cot. Still he could say, 'Ammaji, Ammaji' a couple of times a day. Now that she has also departed, how can he face his empty house? With whom should he share anything? And still he doesn't tell his sorrows to anyone...'

Alongside came phupha's punctuation marks: 'well, friends'...'anyway'...'what's more'...'that's it'...'exactly'.

Suddenly bua would change track. 'And here is this one, who, at the slightest trouble, will announce it to the whole city. I say, keep your troubles at home, the neighbourhood laughs, it does not share in your sorrows. But he...' and she would dilate on phupha's nature.

Phupha would not be prepared for this sudden turn. He would lose his cool, his head would automatically keep nodding 'yes yes' for a while, then he would give an embarrassed smile and with an awkward gesture exit from the scene.

That was the weight that bua put on him. Once he said that laugh who will, I know the hollowness of all these boasts. Every man is a slave to his wife to some extent or the other, and is happy in proportion to his slavery. He gave everyone marks according to his extent of servitude and therefore happiness. He gave himself hundred per cent.

Yet, we heard that there could be arguments between them. One was that bua wanted to come and spend more time with her brother but phupha was not prepared to stay even one day alone, in the care of servants. Bua could thus come only in his vacations. Another cause for a conflict had been that phupha had sent their sons to the hostel against bua's wishes.

But most of all, it seems, the cause of bua's frustration was money. Phupha kept his purse close to him, and ignoring every plea of 'inflation' gave her the same for monthly expenses that he had been giving for the past twenty years. We had ourselves seen phupha's purse stuffed with notes. If by mistake he forgot his wallet, when going to the bathroom or answering dada's call, bua would pounce on it like an eagle and stuff ten or twenty rupees, whatever, into her blouse. Phupha perhaps did not imagine that even dadi would not speak up at such times. Even we, when given money by phupha for chocolates or ice cream, returned the change to bua. Not that she ever asked. We saw her hunting for money, fighting for it, stealing it, and it was clear also that she used it only on the household and not her own clothes or makeup.

Bua would say that she had wanted to complete her BA after her marriage, but could not. Maybe that is why she smiled to see my hopes disappointed, or made a knowing face at my desire to go out. Anyway, she did love me a lot. She made lots of clothes for me.

There is an awareness of nakedness that goes with clothes and began to haunt me at some point in my childhood. Bua disliked open necks, sleeveless outfits, and bare legs. As we were entering the temple she put her shawl over my v-neck pullover. 'An open chest in the temple!' When we were leaving for her mother-in-law's, she brought me back from the doorstep and made me wear a salwar under my frock. A green flower print frock, a blue checked salwar. I was angry at this insult to taste and when mai asked about it on our return, I burst into tears.

All the time, when walking around, bua would pull my dress down, or fix a button, or unroll a sleeve.

With bua I felt as if I was a body.

With bua I felt from my very childhood that I should be wearing a full length veil.

There was a lot of talk about clothes in our house. Dada was not fond of my frocks and pants and such Western attire. Babu was. So I ended up being able to wear all kinds of things. Later Subodh got me to wear bell-bottoms and maxis and midis and god knows what else. I would be wearing a dupatta on my pants and shirt when I left home, and as soon as the gate was crossed, the dupatta would be stuffed into my bag.

We made mai wear a sari with the end over her left shoulder in the modern way. Babu looked at her strangely. Mai put the end over her right shoulder as traditionally done.

I grumbled to myself—mai was looking so nice with her beautiful, moulded figure. There's no shape visible in the *sidha palla*, or 'right end'. It's like being in a sack, wrapped in cloth up to the head. Mai's embroidered blouse with puffed sleeves got hidden.

Babu did not like my wearing a sari even in college. 'You look old,' he would say, 'and the mother and father need to start worrying.' If I had worn a frock even then he would not have minded. As long as it was a full length frock.

Everyone was of one mind on this, that there should be no glimpse of the body. The girl's body. The woman's body.

The body was not a body. It was an invitation to disaster.

Dadi—when she was not ill—fixed her sari end the moment it slipped, even if it was only in front of babu. She wore fine mill-woven saris with her blouses through which peeped her fancy lacy petticoats.

In front of me, on the other hand, there was nothing she would not slip off. 'Just scratch my back a little.'

How many hopes must have been personified in babu for dadi to be so hung up on him! Dada was completely out of reach anyway, whereas babu would pause at her bedside in passing and sit down. He visited dadi at least once a day. The end result of all this was, as expected, that babu became dadi's god. Whenever I see someone crazy with love about another, I remember them. Maybe it my peculiar vision or maybe it is a fundamental truth that, when close-up, different kinds of relationships lose their distinctiveness.

As soon as babu appeared, dadi would brighten up. 'Come, my prince, sit down... where is this mai, is she not going to give something to eat and drink to the poor tired boy?'

'Have some more, son, have some more,' she would persuade him.

If babu ever refused something rich or sweet, she would chide him loudly. 'How will your body keep up? An office-goer needs ghee and sugar. Your keep working off all your strength.'

When babu stood before her he was poor and tired. When he was out of sight he became 'My boy is like an Englishman.'

'Have this, my dear. It's made from home-made ghee. Has anyone ever had indigestion from home-made ghee?'

God, that home-made ghee! That yellow butter and ghee made from cow's milk. In our house everything was made from this real stuff for the longest time. The *gujhia* and *malpua* at Holi, the *gulgule* and *barfi* at Diwali. 'Dalda' cooking oil was bought only at festivals, to make the sweets that would be distributed to servants.

Dadi would keep feeding babu and keep gazing at him with love.

If she said anything to someone else, she would still look at babu and say it. About mai of course, she told babu with particular enthusiasm. But even if she had to tell us, for instance, to eat, she would address babu, 'Here, the children can also eat with you, call them to eat.'

She had to keep talking to babu. She didn't seem to want to keep quiet. Meaningless conversation—'Some termites have appeared on top of the door.' ... 'The dog is barking lot.' ... 'My stomach was rumbling so I had a little *ajvayin*.'

And she would giggle like a little girl if babu ever teased us, maybe by putting on a fake English accent: 'Hello, Mister Shubodd Thewari and you Madam Shunaina Thewari!' As if some lover was flirting with her, Madam Dadi Thewari!

There is a tale that hangs on this 'Tiwari' also. Babaji's ritual had magically stopped me from going to the hostel once, but I had become alert and never took part in any such thing again. For my Master's I went to the hostel. And babu took me to the bank and opened my first savings account so that money could be safely sent from home and not be frittered away. It would be withdrawn only when needed. I was grown up, but the novelty of it made me a child. With pride in signing my name, I began to make a long, artistic signature when babu stopped me at my first name—'That's enough.'

Suddenly I felt small. I asked mai and she explained that if you have to change your name later, why write it? And I felt I don't exist at all, or if Sunaina Tiwari exists it's till the moment of erasure and then she will be a new thing, if she will be at all.

Maybe the parda had fluttered again and the wind had made the flame rise high. 'Tiwari' turned to ashes at that moment. No Tiwari, no changing it, no replacing it. Only Sunaina. And Sunaina would continue.

Even at that moment it did not cross my mind that others similarly had names that had got erased.

We had begun to fight with mai. 'Why don't you say something? Don't you have a will of your own? Don't you think? Why are you afraid? Why are you so weak?'

We were getting strong. We were not afraid. Subodh could talk back to dada without fear. I could wander around in front and when dada said, 'Go inside,' at the opening of the gate, I would go inside. But very slowly, lingering there, my head held high, surveying the visitor with a direct gaze.

There was such urgency to get out of the house. There was this strange pull in the open air.

After I passed Intermediate, I again agitated to leave. Babu brought the application form from the degree college in town. Mai said sadly, you seem so keen to leave home. I kept quiet, defeated, crushed.

If mai did not support me I could not do anything.

Babu said to take English. I said I want to be a doctor, I'll take Biology. Dada furrowed his brow. Dadi laughed, 'hee hee,' sarcastically rolling her eyes in praise of the fifty five percent. Mai repeated babu's opinion, 'There is no future for girls in Science.' And I played the easiest trick on her, 'Is there any future in anything for girls? Who is actually looking for a future in medicine, or in anything else?'

Then mai signed the form. I sneaked out by the back door, jumped over the wire and waited for Subodh. He brought the scooter round to the back and we went and submitted the application form to the college.

Second division...the ruin of her children by mai...the house echoed with ranting against mai. But I at least became a science student in the degree college.

The girls in my college were obsessed with one thing—how to make their bodies invisible within their *dupattas*, and in this process, how to actually make the dupatta invisible and display the body. They would stand and talk with boys at the college gate and laugh and stuff their mouths with their dupattas. There were plenty of boys that could be met: others' brothers, some hanging around at the gate, some cycling alongside the rickshaws. I always left home by the back gate and left mai to worry about confronting babu and dadi.

When Subodh came home some of his friends came too. I would play badminton in the club, go to plays, music programmes, films. There would be an argument with mai to come along. Sometimes we won over her resistance, sometimes she won.

Babu always told mai, 'Stay with them, go along, watch them.' Mai seldom stayed to watch us. Sometimes she would watch a play or film *with* us.

Even if one wanted to, how much could one 'stay with'? The college, library, and so on apart, mai even kept the back door open. Subodh did not hesitate in speaking to my girlfriends in front of mai, nor I in talking to his friends. Yet, if babu came in, my tongue would turn to stone. Even if he sat in the nearby room, my eyes would look down and lips fall still and our general noise lessen, if not subside completely.

After Subodh went back to the hostel his friend continued to bring and take books. If this friend met babu he would have a chat about Subodh and go back. If he did not, then he would enter by the backdoor, laugh and greet dadi and go to mai. I would go there also.

Once he brought me a book. Babu asked him, 'What is it?' 'Sunaina wanted to read it,' he said. 'Give it to me,' said babu. Babu took the book from his hand and he tried in vain to remove a piece of paper from inside. The book had already changed hands. Babu opened the paper. It was a long composition. He closed it and told his usual lie, 'Right, Sunaina is not at home right now, I'll give it to her.'

I was ready to die. Babu did not even look at me, just told mai, 'It was Ramesh...What is the book? *For Whom the Bell Tolls.*' He handed the paper separately, 'Have a look. What is it?'

Mai saw my name on it. 'For you.' She handed it to me. Her voice was indifferent.

I read the love poem, read the breathless expression of youth. Believing that something huge and dramatic was transpiring, that I was holding the key to someone's life or death, I said gravely, 'Everything seems so difficult mai, I'll tell you everything sometime.'

Mai never asked. I fell on the bed and sobbed, 'Oh no no no, he loves me so.' I was fully in sympathy with the poor soul's suffering. For myself I did not want to pause anywhere right now, I could not give him anything, I would fly away, any minute, far away.

Dada also saw him one time and boomed, 'Who are you, whom do you want to meet?'

He began to stammer, 'That...book of Sunaina's...'

'Sunaina,' dada thundered.

I came.

'Who is this?'

My tongue betrayed me. 'I don't know.'

I never forgave dada for making me tell a lie.

But Ramesh forgave me. By the time I went to the hostel for my MA, he had begun to meet me in the club, the Company Gardens, here and there. We became close before my departure. My first kiss, trembling in the onset of youth...

Subodh knew some of these things. In any case, the two-year difference between us ensured that the aches of new experiences would be the same. We were growing up together. Youth had the upper hand, both inside and outside the house, in spite of babu's 'stay with them' to mai, dada's 'go inside' to us, and dadi's 'cover your legs' to me. Life cannot be extinguished in a closed room. Youth, in its turn, is a gas balloon that flies crazily even if held by a string, and if the string is let go, then the balloon reaches the clouds.

We talked to each other a lot. About everything. We would solemnly exchange views on sex on the roof. If it was dirty or pure, how one could ever let oneself be trespassed thus, if love was only lust, if love could exist without sex, if love was the real thing only without sex...If...If...Seriousness came easily then. We could forget everything else and be aware only of the rising and falling swell of our questionings. We would be in the depths of seriousness, our faces wearing a suitable tension, purposefully pushing away the amusement that threatened. Till an ordinary happening like our sneezing together or a rickshawalla's cry from the far road—'Bhaiya, move a bit to the side'—made the balloon burst. Our solemnity would hiss out and we would roar with laughter as if some terrifically amusing incident had taken place.

There were also those crude jokes very popular in our friends' circles. Such as the one about mosquitoes flooding into the ship. They were biting everyone and a young woman lifted her top—'Do these look like mosquito bites to you?'

Once mai reached upstairs with a snack so we told her the joke as well. She smiled but commented that it wasn't funny. Just bringing up a forbidden subject did not make it funny. Then she told us this story about when earthlings met people from another planet. The outsiders were showing off their ways to the earthlings, this is how we do this, this is how we do that, and this is how we produce a baby in two minutes. Then the earthlings boasted about their ways, how they do this, that, and the other, and how they produce a baby in nine months. The people from outer space were astounded at this—if it takes you nine months then why are you in such a hurry in the beginning?

We laughed our heads off. Mai had heard it with babu at the club. We laughed more because it was mai who narrated it. Our hearts rejoiced at this sign that somehow we three made a team.

But no one admits the fullness of each moment even to oneself, let alone to others. We certainly did not tell mai, or even each other, every single thing. I knew that Subodh had secrets. I knew that Ranjana and Anjan's older sister, didi, let him get on top of her in bed. When Subodh came home for the holidays she would spend the night at our house. We slept out in the courtyard in summer, surrounded by the fragrance of *madhumalati* and *chameli*. Dada and babu would spread out in the front room before a table fan. Mai slept with us. We were in a line, mai, then I, then Subodh, then Anjan, then Ranjana, then didi in the corner. She would find an excuse to pull Subodh's head lovingly to her ample breast. Subodh had once told me that after he fell asleep she came to his bed and put his hand in her kurta.

I did not tell mai all this. I did not even tell mai that the fat, greasy Beri maharaj who came to meet babu, who called me to him with 'Come here, daughter,' tried to caress my breasts under the cover of innocently holding my arm. Once he called and asked me to read some numbers he claimed he couldn't read. I read them in English and he said, 'In Hindi, daughter.' I read 1722 in Hindi, '*ek sat do do,'* or, 'the two of us together.' He went on laughing and his eyes were two burning coals. Mai did not understand why I tried to avoid him and why Subodh leapt on him like a ferocious dog.

Dada or babu would never let us go anywhere. It was impossible to spend the night somewhere. They had a particular fear of the night. I am not sure who they tried to save us from.

Babu and dada and dadi tried to cover us up everywhere, to ensure that we would not see something and that something of ours would not be seen.

Once didi—yes, the same didi—arrived with her new baby and mai kissed him on the mouth.

Babu was shocked. 'Oh...no...' His voice was not angry but full of criticism. 'In front of the children,' he told didi.

Maybe he thought we would begin grabbing people and kissing them on the mouth.

Once some guest of dada's clinked his sharbat glass with Subodh's and said 'Cheers'. Dada was furious—'One shouldn't even joke like that before children. The very thought of it should not enter their minds.'

Our style was that at night before mai we would clink our water glasses dozens of times—'Cheers.' We were constantly puffing away at the candy cigarettes that babu brought.

We did not have much of a tradition of drinking or offering drinks, however. There were tales of dada drinking at one time. He had some narratives of 'wining and dining' with his English friends. Babu drank in the club and sometimes in his room with phuphaji or another guest, or even alone maybe, but away from our eyes. After dada and dadi passed away he did sometimes have his 'medicine' outside his room.

The odd thing is that we actually thought it was 'medicine' in our childhood. We did not think at all that it was alcohol. The word 'liquor' itself was forbidden in our house, like the words 'shit' and 'piss'. What we did was 'big bathroom' and 'small bathroom'.

In front of us even Hardeyi and Bhondu did only that, what they did on their own was anybody's guess. Thus the word 'liquor' was never pronounced.

Odder is that we never said 'medicine' either. The 'medicine' was kept locked in the clothes almirah in babu's room. Mai occasionally took it out and gave it to Hardeyi, who gave it to Bhondu, who took it on a tray with water and ice to the front sitting room where now babu and his cronies gathered. When Hardeyi passed by us, she felt provoked by our staring eyes to hide the 'medicine' further with her sari.

I did not ever hear anyone say that the 'medicine' was a bad thing but I knew well that I would never be given it. Somehow I knew it was bitter. I knew it smelt. There was some mystery in the air about it. That explains why when sitting with bua one day and while Hardeyi and mai were shifting babu's almirah and there was a loud noise of a bottle breaking inside and a dark, smelly liquid began to flow out, we both became embarrassed and murmuring defensively, 'What is this strange thing...' went up to the roof in case we were given an answer.

I had even found, late at night, a smelly, empty glass next to mai when babu was not in the house.

I don't know what I must have thought in those childhood days because I did not then reflect on whatever I thought. We saw some films and plays, read books, and sometimes in fun, painting beards and moustaches with ink on our faces, we would down glasses of water and falter—tongues slurring, steps falling, eyes rolling—playacting and giggling.

While playacting we did not consciously think that there was actual liquor around, or connect liquor with 'medicine', or 'medicine' with babu, or babu with mai, or mai with a smell that came from a glass, or the smell with a wind that blew in from somewhere into someone's life.

All we connected was mai and ourselves. We poured ourselves into her empty shell. We tried to fill her weak, cowardly self with our bravado.

Gradually we became like watchdogs for mai, standing on guard near her. In our earlier, scared days, if anyone said anything to her, we would look up swiftly, our eyes full of worry and sympathy. Now we started growling. Then, as occasion demanded, barking. If needed, we were ready to take the next step—biting.

We had begun to be afraid for mai. We wanted to get her out with us.

The day she fell down we were really afraid. Our hearts began to beat hard, and continued to do so.

Mai had become unconscious, she was raised and put on a bed, babu ran for the doctor, dada began to circle around, dadi began to moan.

Mai was in bed ill.

I don't remember her ever being ill before. I only remember her working, bent over, listening and accepting everything. If she ever had a headache during one of her many fasts, her face would grimace slightly, her colour fade somewhat. But she would continue to work like before. That she must have had a headache on other days too was clear when she refused aspirin or saridon on her fast days. Meaning that she was familiar with these pills. But as the headaches did not change her routine, I forgot about them. Hence the belief that mai had never been ill before. It was only dadi's right to complain about once a month—'Oh god, oh god, take me, take me, I cannot bear the pain...'

So when mai fell we were speechless.

She told us that suddenly her legs had started to tremble, that often they hurt and so did her back.

The doctor checked her back, told babu that an X-ray was needed, but not right away. That first mai should lie on a hard wooden bed, not one of string or cotton belt, without a pillow, and take pills for both her back and her leg ache. This is not an illness, the doctor said consolingly, it happens because of bending.

Dadi repeated this statement countless times that this is not an illness, it has happened because of bending. There was sympathy and relief in her voice but also resentment about why, if it was not an illness, there should be so much concern and flitting around mai.

Babu was tireless in running errands for mai, to the hospital, bazaar, everywhere. Dadi's heart would melt looking at him—'Oh dear, see how much work has come on my poor son. He has to attend to the office, to the home, do all the running around for the doctor, oh, he looks so exhausted.'

There was the poor son and then there was the poor son's mother! Because now for the first time dadi felt the burden of the kitchen. I had my classes in the morning. Hardeyi didn't have the right touch. So dadi had to get to and either do or have everything done.

Dadi made a delectable meal. With ghee in abundance. She made lighter but delicious things for mai—tapioca, gourds, *parval* juice, *khichari* of *mung dal*.

Her voice was audible the whole day—'Oh, you fool, you've put so much cumin? Four annas' worth in one go?'

'Oh oh oh, you are not looking, idiot, the milk has boiled over. I can smell it from here. At least one rupee wasted.'

'Oh, such damage...is it your man's money?'

There was an accounting the whole day of how much money Hardeyi had swallowed, how much Bhondu had gobbled up. Then again for the meals she served them twice a day.

'You all won't eat it, so I have to give the morning's dal to them. It has at least a *chhatak*'s worth of ghee.'

'Such expensive spinach, ground on a stone that was deliberately not washed clean. It's gritty and the whole thing has to be given to them. What luxury for them!'

Mai needed complete rest. The doctor said that she suffered a lot of pain. When she was allowed up, babu borrowed a car to take her to the hospital for an X-ray.

The doctor said that this was the fate of those who work bending over. The substance between the vertebrae got eroded by constant bending and produced wrong pressure on the nerves. That such people had pain when they bent over and pain when they straightened up.

In medical terms the doctor explained that the disc cushion that joined the vertebrae in the spinal column had eroded. There was a substance called 'annulus fibrosus' on the outside, and a soft gelatinous substance called 'nucleus pulposus' inside. This cushion gave the spine flexibility, but the disc could wear away from sitting in faulty postures, standing and working too long, and from straining. The vertebrae shifted from their position, got crooked, and pressed on the nerves.

The doctor said that the pain would continue. Yes, she could wear a 'belt', do the exercises he advised, rest periodically, and take painkillers when it got bad.

'This is not an illness,' the doctor added. 'It is common in women.'

Dadi breathed a sigh of relief and repeated this. She said that we children would never remember what had fallen to *her* lot, the artificial joint and the limping around.

And we? We knew from the beginning that mai had a weak spine.

We kept pitying her weakness, saving her, and then one day even felt a little repulsed by her helplessness.

One day escapes from me just now, but I cannot say what day that must have been.

It must have stretched over a long time but when I try to remember it, it seems that suddenly so much changed in the house. Mai began to walk with a belt, but walk more than before. Because now she walked outside the house as well, and in the front, inhabited now only by dada's memory. She walked around inside where dadi's interference had vanished with dadi.

As mai became old she became the mistress of the house in one stroke.

Dadi died as an auspicious married woman. She was fond of saying—"I have only one prayer to the lord, that he take me before he takes him.' Her chin, its bone weathered away ages ago, would shake when her lips trembled. I felt like laughing about how she had nothing to do with dada *now*, while he was alive.

Dadi was a determined person. Pushing the doctor's restrictions far away she kept eating, slyly, boldly, and did not lose days from her life. She died in her own time and died well after passing seventy. Now if someone tells me that one dies at the time that is right for one, I don't laugh. Anyway, dadi died, dada was inconsolable, and then he also departed after a few years.

I don't remember all this clearly. I remember the flowers, the pandit's words, the crowd. I remember that the day dada or dadi died, I was supposed to go to some event in the club and was sorry that I couldn't go. It was dark and I was outside and I saw babu hurrying home. I knew it was him but in the dark only his white clothes could be seen, as if he was a headless ghost, and I came inside. Then I remember that one day one of us said that if you stare at dada's photo in the sitting room you will hear his footsteps behind and I began to go to the sitting room to see. And I remember that I had come alone up to the roof to see dadi's blue bolster pillowcase drying on the clothesline, and I cried.

Mai began to talk to the servants and labourers. The *mehndi* bushes in front of dada's sitting room, which used to fill with white flowers and green buds in March and the leaves of which we ground and used for artwork on our palms, were trimmed. The wild grass growing within the mehndi bushes was pulled out and taken away in bundles. The earth there was dug up, a roller was run on it, grass was planted there in the monsoon and mai's lawn was inaugurated. Flowerbeds were made and English roses started blooming. More flowerbeds were made and different varieties of blooms nodded away—candytuft, flox, petunia, nasturtium.

There was a sitting place on the lawn which, according to dada, snakes could reach via the long grass surrounding it. Now it was sprinkled with water by the *bhishti* everyday and Bhondu would put four armchairs and a round table. A tablecloth would be spread and a copper vase placed. Babu would get tea there for his visitors. *Sharbat* became less popular.

If no one came, mai would sit there with her sewing or knitting. The labourers came to her for instructions. I would sit near her doing something. If the gate opened mai promptly rose and went inside.

The movement between inside and outside increased. One may even say that mai was more visible outside than inside—on the lawn, in the fields, bent over flower-pots and beds.

I remember not so much how dada and dadi passed away but more how it was at home after them, in the new season of moderation.

The prison walls of the kitchen also opened up. Babu had stomach trouble anyway and ate little, ate simple. But no so little that mai could sit idle. There may have been no kachoris or pakoris but there was simple *chura matar*, and there was fruit chat. Ready-made snacks from the market also made it easier. If there was a sudden demand from babu's friends, biscuits, *dalmoth*, squash, and tea could be sent out to them.

Mai's world expanded.

On newly-minted, gleaming mornings, mai, her sari end over her head, would be giving orders in the field, plucking *gurhal*, *gainda*, and *bela* on a washed banana leaf for puja, or watering her plants using the hosepipe, or breaking off dried leaves.

Once we were sitting with her on the boundary wall of the fragrant mustard field.

'Aren't they beautiful mai,' Subodh had come home. 'Plants always bring happiness.'

'Not always.' Mai was teasing. 'The papaya plant doesn't bring happiness. It is male, it doesn't bear flowers.'

The house was surrounded by plenty of land. Eight or ten acres of wheat, *arhar*, corn, with ripe golden heads in April. There were vegetables behind the courtyard. And trees of banana, *amla*, *barhar*, *champa*, papaya, lime, and jackfruit. Bunches of banana would be hung in the rooms here and there, everywhere, to ripen—a jump, a leap, and you have a fruit in your hand!

There were bushes too of *karonda* at the back, from which mai made pickle like only she could.

Mai had poles fixed in front of the sitting room and grape vines planted. In May and June there were luscious green bunches.

The fields had been dada's responsibility before. There were vegetables, greens, cereals, mangoes, guavas at the time. Jackfruit dishes and pickles were made even then. But when mai put her touch on the garden, there was a new womanly blossoming.

In the days 'after' the 'before' I saw mai peaceful but withdrawn.
If I got up early I was also touched by the pure greeting of the
morning. A sweet gentleness with the cooing of the cuckoo and
the song of the birds. The mild smell of the lime trees mingling
with the fragrance of *harshringar*, roses, *chameli*. A cool, fresh
breeze and an innocence burgeoning everywhere. Far away at
distant well the oxen would be yoked and the sweet smell of their
hay and their dung would arise. There was the sound of sweeping
in front of the servants' homes and people could be seen brushing
their teeth with lime twigs. Mai, her eyes soft, was a part of these
lovely mornings.

I still could not believe, however, that all was well for mai.
Whether wood or coal or gas stove, it was essentially the same
story repeated all over again.

I had come outside the gates myself. I had to get her out now.
Dada had said, the world outside the gates is poisoned, keep safely
away from it. The question had already hit me—how did you
manage? What kind of poison is this that no one else can survive it
but you? If we are so different because we are children, how about
mai and dadi? Why are they so vulnerable that they also have to
keep themselves safe inside?

I was no longer a child. My childhood was gone, dada and
dadi were gone. We had left the house and babu could never bring
us back in by himself. Now the back gate was also little used—
Bhondu had no coals to bring in a sack, and I had nowhere to go in
secret after telling only mai. No longer did the occasion arise that
babu saw me and said, 'You should ask,' and I said, 'I did ask mai,'
but, afraid that mai would be scolded, added the lie that I had to
study for the exams and my girlfriend picked me up in her car, and
that's why mai permitted me to go.

Those days were gone. But the days when we imagined that
we saved mai and we *had* to save mai were still there.

So when we could not save her, we would grumble that mai would not cooperate. While on her way out with us, if she exchanged a glance with babu, she would suddenly turn right back, even if it meant throwing cold water on some plans we made specifically for her.

Thus, after much pleading, we finally won her over to go with us to some friends in the mountains. She had panicked, but her face had flushed a little in excitement. She had asked if such-and-such a temple was nearby and we had told her it was just an hour away by taxi and a great pilgrimage place. We told babu about it in a stern voice. We told him that there was no room for bargaining or deals, that everything was settled and we were going to buy the tickets. After we got them mai kept saying, 'Return the tickets. You can go, I am not forbidding you. I don't feel like it, so what will be the use?'

Subodh began to mutter, 'Who can do anything against someone's will? She does not want it, she herself will not cooperate with us. Suni, she is such a weakling.'

Suni and Subodh were no longer 'weaklings'. They had isolated themselves, and when you are alone you have to answer only to yourself. After that, when you have only yourself to think of, you become extra special. You are the strongest, the cleverest, the greatest, able to do battle with everything. So why waste your specialness on simple, straightforward matters? The more difficult and complicated the business, the better for the self. Huge battles. Giant victories. Thunderous defeats.

But maybe I had become neither so independent, nor so 'myself'. When I came home in the holidays and babu passed on my letters to me opened, I was unable to say anything for days. I kept reading the opened letters addressed to me, a storm raging inside me.

One day something must have happened that may have had nothing to do with letters or with anything at all. Something made my voice falter and my tears flow, and then one tear led to another and I seemed to remember many things that made me tearful and they fell like a thundershower. I was beside myself with weeping. Mai, worried, held me. Babu came running. I somehow stammered—'He has no faith...he opens my letters...' Mai looked questioningly at babu. Babu, embarrassed, said—'Oh, all right...I must have opened them by mistake...all right, all right...'

I had also opened a letter by mistake. It was in the picture frame on mai's shelf for her hair oil and comb. Subodh had bought a camera and taken dozens of pictures of everyone and I wanted to frame dada and dadi's. I opened up the photo frame. Out came the piece of paper, addressed to mai.

I had never wondered that mai didn't get any letters addressed to her. Ever. Now, perversely, I wondered about this one letter addressed to her. A letter to her?

By mistake I had opened that letter which I had then not understood. Not understood who it was that thought of her, would always think of her, who only wished her the best in her married life, who would keep going 'home' and getting news of her, who wanted every happiness in life for her and if at any point suddenly met her would know from her happiness that it was she, the same, my very own, and then yours-something a-jumbled-up-signature.

The yellow, crumbling paper seemed to burn my fingers and I quickly buried it again in the papers on the frame.

I did not ever have the courage to disturb the meditative calm on mai's face.

Subodh kept moving out easily from the house. He did not have to plead or fight. After graduating from the Englishmen's boarding school he went to do his BA in another university in an even bigger town. He started enquiries there and I also arrived, to do my MA. We were in separate hostels and colleges but once again as if in one 'school'. Then Subodh went away to England.

I give Subodh the credit for getting me out of the house. He had always fought for me, against dada, dadi, and babu. I could only sit to one side and keep crying. Mai would sit quietly, looking at one, then at another, listening to one side, then the other.

Subodh would not budge.

Dada would scream, 'Her brother has come first in the state, what has she done that she is jumping around to go out and study? We are not prepared to spoil our children's future by sending them to strange places. Everyone's daughters study here, are they all out of their minds?' Babu cried. Subodh asked—'Suni, is this some sort of a performance?' Mai said a lot to me separately—'Think about it Suni, if something happens to babu...? I want that you should achieve something, make a name. But think about it carefully. Is it necessary to leave? You both are grown-up now. You understand the world. How would I know which place is best for what? You are so keen to leave. Think about it. Why?'

And I would become exhausted from the self-questioning expected of me. How keen am I really? ... Truly it is no small thing to do an MA there... What will I become? ... Can I become anything?

Where is the scale to be found that would enable me to weigh to the last pound, ounce, and fraction thereof, my longing to go away against rationality? But even if that scale could be found, why do you make me weigh everything so carefully?

'She will learn many kinds of things there, mai, her confidence will grow, studies are not everything,' Subodh kept explaining in a determined voice. 'Here you have the same old, worn-out studies and the timid, cowering girls.'

'Women fall into bad ways outside the house,' screamed the voices echoing against the walls. Mai retreated into a decisive silence. Babu kept at her. 'Do something. They listen to you. You have spoiled them so much that they listen to no one else. Entreat, threaten, explain, persuade. Save the family from ruin. Fall at her feet and plead. Hit her. You are the mother, you have the right... they will listen to you...'

Babu understood this deep truth about whom we would listen to. But we did not understand as much. I thought I left because Subodh got me out. He was the one who met everyone face to face. Mai did not speak. She did nothing.

I had no time to think that maybe the credit also went to her who refused to become the echo of someone else's voice, who simply heard impassively what everyone said. It was beyond my understanding that if mai had said once, 'Forget it, Sunaina,' Sunaina's legs would have become paralysed and Subodh would be left muttering helplessly.

Mai remained silent.

I left.

Dadi and dada passed away.

Babu kept blaming mai all his life.

We were angry with him—'Why do you blame mai? We are responsible for doing this.'

Subodh was younger but had seen the world, travelled around alone, met all kinds of people, driven babu's scooter. Dada and dadi treated his opinions like adult ones. It was totally within his capacity, to be able to get me out.

I left the house crying. But as we sat in the train, the man opposite took off his shoes, put his wallet inside one, made a pillow of them, and we burst out laughing. The excitement of being able to start a new life could not but touch me. When the train started the house was left far behind. Ahead was the impatient, calling flutter of thousands and thousands of birds.

I probably did not miss home that first time. A wealth of freshly minted coins was pouring into my lap in a rush. On the one hand there was hesitation and fear, on the other thrill and enthusiasm. There was fear in everything, there was attraction in everything. For days it seemed only a role in a play where I was alone and an adult. Cross the road after looking both ways, stand on your toes and push back the flap of the letter box and put your hand inside to post a letter for mai, then rehearse to yourself in the autorickshaw—'Go to. ... How much? ... Here you are.' There was happiness even in meeting so many unknown girls washing faces and brushing teeth in the morning.

We had 'ragging' in our hostel. My underpants, which mai used to sew—white cotton, with lace, and a cord—were furled like a flag on a tall pole and I marched left-right left-right holding the pole. Whenever they pleased, the seniors would stop me—'Halt, one two! Attention...what is this fresher?'

'My underpants.'

I had a laugh too and wrote everything to mai in detail.

Subodh was in another college. He had fewer rules and regulations so it was usually he who visited me. I could write a whole book on our rules. Everything was fixed—the times at which you could leave, the number of times a week, the time allowed out on holidays, what was permitted, what was forbidden, ask in advance, show the warden the permission slip, don't go alone if not to your local guardian's house, if there, then show a signed slip, give a report on every breath of every pore, every drop of sweat, and every movement.

Very soon we all became our own 'local guardians' and could present as many signatures as needed. Or we would leave together, part and go our separate ways, and then return together. We were certainly nervous at the thought of bumping into any of our lawmakers in the market. But it was a large city that encompassed the whole world on all sides, seemingly without limits. Just like our courage.

Our security was assured by an attendance roll taken at half past eight in the evening, after which the guard would immediately close the one main entrance—the college gate was some distance away—of the hostel. From the outside.

Inside there were rooms all around a courtyard. The main door had a window of one and a half foot square out of which one could put one's head and shout, 'Chaukidar! Chaukidar!' There were sparks from the electric cable once and we all crowded near the door like frightened sheep and kept shouting, 'Open the door, there's going to be a fire!'

There was every possible kind of rule here to save us. Cigarette smokers would be expelled (God knows who used to put a pile of cigarette butts in the dustbin). Those who went around with boys... (there were romances upon romances, in spite of the glass-studded walls and the one and a half foot square windows). This-no, that-yes. Or, this-yes, that-no.

Once there was a love letter for me from an admirer, I know not who, saying that in your blue eyes I have found not only beauty, but also intelligence, and whichever day I catch sight of you is a blessed one, and when I don't see you I want to kill myself. You did not come to play badminton the day before yesterday. Won't you play badminton with me, won't you meet me? Only for an intellectual friendship, not romance, as Ghalib says... My would-be lover quoted the poet. I showed my friends the letter.

If it were not for the blue eyes and the Ghalib, I might definitely have become interested. Now I stood guilty with my head bowed down in the principal's office, the letter on her desk. Subodh, being specially summoned, was standing to one side, and lover boy was lost somewhere in some dream of blue eyes.

I got a 'warning'.

I told mai. She wrote back, worried. Take care. Don't do anything that would permit a finger to be lifted at you. But if people say incorrect things then don't bother about them, just worry about yourself. And write about what else you need, how much money. Have you stitched the buttons on your shirt or are you managing with a safety pin? Look after each other. When are your coming? Subodh writes that he will have to stay on for two or three days; how will you come alone?

Whatever happened, no one could curb my exuberance any more. My thoughts now and then could be wrung by the memory of mai but when I thought of the house, it was as if I remembered a prison.

In the holidays we came home to mai. I also came and went now like Subodh. We stood together at the station waiting for the train, our suitcases full of presents for everyone, as eager as the huge rats that frolicked in the garbage between the rails.

I had reached the hostel. Subodh by talking, and mai by keeping quiet, had got me there. So that I could grow. Become something.

I think of the doll that I once started making in my crafts class with the enthusiasm that accompanies mastering new skills. I made the hands. I made the feet. I made the trunk. I stuffed them with cotton and sewed them up. I made the whole body, well-balanced and nice. By the time it came to attaching the head I began to tire. The trunk separate, the head separate, the doll was dumped somewhere.

We kept going home for all the holidays, Holi, Diwali, and so on, to mai, carrying the outside world's exuberance with us. But something had begun to change, unnoticed.

It was not that our plans to rescue mai could be shaken. They had not been that precise. Yes, they certainly still existed: we would finish our studies, start earning, then mai would stay now with Subodh, now with me.

When we went home we took her out much more than before. We lectured her on how to handle everything outside the house. After all, we had ourselves learnt how to board a bus, buy tickets, buy anything, only after we had left home.

We could see that it would take time for mai to learn to function in the world. Pulled and pushed by us to the outside, mai became a little girl. She crossed the road holding our hands, entered a crowd frightened, and wherever possible tried to hide behind us and make herself invisible.

Our town was small but did belong to this century. Its continuous progress is not easy to describe. New objects pushing out old ones. The first one not discarded yet while the second arrived. Then the third, the fourth. By the time the tenth came someone calculated that the second one had more disadvantages than advantages, but by then too many wrong turns had been taken.

There was no question that our small town had to be progressive. This was quite clear from the varieties of cinema halls we had. New, grand buildings with amazing lights, airconditioners that worked from the time of entry to the beginning of the movie, and elevators. Mai entered these in a panic and at each floor as the door opened, her body strained with tension to run outside!

As luck would have it, mai, with this instinct, had to be the one to get stuck in the elevator. The electricity failed and mai, I, and a small child were between two floors in the dark and the heat. I feel suffocated thinking of it. It was chokingly dark, a veritable hell, and I started banging on the door hysterically and crying out. Then the light came on but the elevator stayed where it was, in space. The ten- or twelve-year-old boy kept crying, 'O god, my god, what about mummy and papa, how will they know?' It seemed our shouts could not reach the distant crowds. There was the chaos of the film itself. Mai took the child's hand and told him that her son was waiting upstairs with the tickets, he knew that we were here and would have the door opened, calling the mechanic if necessary. Then I began to call out in a clear voice, 'We are in the lift here. Is there anyone there? Subodh?'

Mai, if taken out somewhere, could become most nervous not just about elevators, but about toilets. That they were dirty was part of the problem of course. She opened the toilet door with a push of her foot and came out using almost no hands, maybe two fingers, then rubbed her hands with maybe a drop of water. But it was part of a bigger nervousness that made her keep sitting in her place rather than go to the toilet. Before leaving the house she would be closeted in the bathroom for some time. In spite of that if she did have to go while we were out, mai would plead— 'Please come with me!' 'No,' we would say strictly, 'go by yourself, you know where it is.' She would fidget and plead, 'No, I won't remember by myself. Come with me. Only this time. Never again.'

Similarly, once we scolded her and stood her at the ticket window—'*You* buy the tickets. Because you get nervous. This will cure you.' She began to stammer like a child—'I can do it if I have to, but why now?' But the two of us did not give in. She tried to scare us, 'Then I won't go with you both.' We still did not give in. Finally she went and stood at the counter with money in her hands.

But as soon as the man said, 'Yes?' she became dumb. She turned a face towards us that defied all description and Subodh said, in spite of himself, 'Three, balcony.'

That was the mai that we had started to teach, whom we were obsessed with giving a chance to live. Our fists were still clutched around our childhood plan—save her, get her out.

But there was something that was changing silently. Or it changed later, or later than later. In a very subtle way. Otherwise we would have stopped it, wouldn't we? There appeared the slightest hint of looking down upon, a kind of impatience, a strange irritation in our concern for mai.

We had escaped. We were free to fly in vast open spaces. We had learnt so much. Now even I knew what Ganpat Rai really was: a disease. We had used our scales and decided what in the world to call 'justice', 'injustice', 'equality', and 'inequality'. We were obsessed with our own vision of humanitarianism and whatever we saw was through the efflorescence of our lenses. The objects which had the tint of our efflorescence looked lovely. Only such objects could attract us and we looked around for them.

If mai's image seemed to change because of her own stubbornness, we became shaken.

We considered ourselves right, so whoever was not completely like us but like something else could only be mistaken. And wrong.

Mai, after all, was not like us.

Mai did parda. And as I said, mai being in parda did not mean for us that there was a real person who did parda. This did not strike us. For us the parda was the only reality.

We had despised this parda from our childhood. Some tiny fragment of that despising got mixed up in our pity for mai.

She simply refused to understand. She refused to change, to escape. We would fight for her again and again, and she would betray us. Babu, from whom we scurried around trying to save her, was exactly the one she would submit to. She could at best dust him off only from his discarded shirt and pants, as she did everyday when he stepped out of them.

She was trapped. She was in chains.

Although now mai, too, began to have guests. Many of those who visited our house after dada and dadi's time brought their wives along.

Mai had begun to speak more than before. Even babu had begun to speak as never before. As if death had opened the gates of a jail. Mai also began to go places with babu more often.

At the same time the whispering at night increased. It's a pity that we were grown up and could not just call out. Still we would be restless because we were sure that mai was unhappy. We worried but controlled ourselves. It seemed that there was sorrow and pain in the whispering, and subdued anger.

Mai and babu did not have fights. Even the fights that resounded in the house with us as subjects did not bring them face to face or into an exchange of query and response. We never saw them fight.

Or love.

But we began to see them together. In the presence of others, to even laugh or talk together. But by themselves—leaving aside the mystery of the night—they were never together. Their rooms were still apart. When we came we stayed in mai's room—our childhood room—with her.

And yet mai was bent over as before for babu. Grinding, cooking, fixing something. We scolded, reminded mai about her back, but mai turned a deaf ear to us. Babu's will, before it could become a command, was always done.

So much so that if we showed indifference to babu, mai's face would show pain. She would say, 'Now you are grown up. You live on your own. What can one tell you? You know what's best for you.'

Subodh had begun to call babu feudal and scold him for his conservative views—'You say without a thought that x number of people have arrived and will all eat here. Have you ever thought about how the person inside will manage, or if she is well? Your health is so dear to you that you must be regular about your yoga and god knows what else. Have you ever given a thought to the health of those inside?'

Babu would say nothing but mai's eyes would flash with the weight of humiliation—'I don't ask you to become like me, why do you want to forcefully change me? My world might be founded on sand and will crumble on its own, why are you kicking it?'

Once babu, in a completely innocent voice, called mai ignorant. Our childhood memories were awakened. Then too she had been called 'ignorant' in the club on one occasion. Today could we quietly accept this talk of knowledge and ignorance? We were provoked. 'It's you who, outwardly educated, are ignorant and superstitious.' And added in English—'You talk like a foolish illiterate.'

Mai was angry. 'Have you been given permission to say any nonsense your like in English? If you cannot respect your father, you don't need to come home. Stay in England or wherever you like.'

Mai opposing us? We could have cried. How could we save someone who wanted to remain tied to her post?

'An ignorant person cannot be transformed into a wise one'—was a thought that was not spoken, nor was it clearly worded. But in our solitude, watching the sunset across the silent fields from the roof, this feeling had insinuated itself into our wordless thoughts.

We would never have accepted babu's calling mai 'ignorant' but we ourselves were thinking something similar. We were the ones who opposed babu on this. We had announced about something that 'mai does not think like this.' Babu replied authoritatively, glancing behind us, to our right and to our left, that one who has no knowledge or experience of the world, can think any odd thing she likes. There may be no orthodoxy in her views but there was no maturity either. That is why, he said, you children get away with teaching her anything you like.

Teaching mai was certainly a task before us. A huge one.

Mai still moved around the house like a shadow, bent over but looking lovely. She was busy but with new things now. She would get magazines of needlecraft, knitting, and farming. The wives of the servants began visiting from the back. They stitched clothes with mai or knitted sweaters and shawls. Mai had her covered baskets on the verandah with thread, wool, and yarn.

The age of television had arrived. When babu was not around the servants' women and children arrived to see Hindi films. The sweeper woman would romp in with her platoon of children.

In dadi's reign this would have been inconceivable. She could literally smell a sweeper from a distance—'What if the government has made them equal? Do they rub scent on their bodies now?'

Mai never said anything to us about sweepers. Their wives and children sat a little apart from others and watched television. But when Hardeyi went off to her village, mai, without telling babu, had the bejewelled daughter-in-law of the aged sweepress scrub her hands with soap and wash the clothes till Hardeyi returned.

Mai did all this while remaining a shadow, did it neither like a thief nor like a heroine.

It may have been that mai had no knowledge or experience of the world, but she had launched into new things. She had thrown herself into social service with the other wives at the club. A fête was organised in the club, stalls were set up, and the housewives became shopkeepers. Mai sold carrot halwa. There was lucky dip, raffle, music, lights, and so on. The money earned was all sent off to the widows' home.

When the war started a plan was made to build up the soldiers' courage. The housewives made garlands of flowers, hot tea in large kettles, *puris* and *cholas* and went off to the train station. The soldiers got off smiling in their khaki uniforms and the women put *tika* on their foreheads, tied *rakhis*, garlanded them, gave them food and tea and sent them off to battle.

One time these women even organised a fashion show in the club after reading *Femina*, *Eve's Weekly*, and so on. We were not there but mai told me and indeed demonstrated how the girls who were models came swaying on to the stage, spun around like tops, threw open their sari ends and turning their necks at an angle, gave a lightning smile.

But our gaze had become fixed and could only see the image that was caught in it from childhood. What we could see was a bent over, defeated shadow cooking something over a fire and getting burnt as she did so.

We would get after her. 'Leave all this. Read instead.' 'Let me finish the work,' she would say, 'then I can enjoy reading.' 'Where's the need for so much fuss?' we would insist. 'Enough that you have made one or two things. Why do you need now to grind chutney, roast papads, make a yogurt salad, have a dessert?'

Then she would hide her fussing from us and do it secretly. Just as everyone runs to look for a naughty child if he is suddenly silent, we would jump up to find mai if we noticed that we could neither hear nor see her.

We would indeed be right. She would be discovered, her door shut softly, grinding a chutney, or mashing up boiled greens, or something.

We would laugh. Scold. Despise her for it.

But what really put us off was seeing her with babu. She never spoke loudly to him, hardly looked straight at him, but there was a special attitude only for him. If she had to tell us to give something to babu, there was the same tone—sighing suffering, full of martyrdom.

There was another thing. If anyone came to meet babu she would tell us to lower the volume on our record player. Then she would seem to concentrate on her knitting or embroidery, but as long as the visitors were in the sitting room she was all ears. And suppose babu, in the midst of his talk about politics, commented how no one could be trusted nowadays—they said sweet things but carried a knife to kill you—then mai would sigh as if she was being pointed at. If babu discoursed on the law and on how even a blood tie did not give the right to grab another's possessions; if even his own kith and kin attacked him, wouldn't he raise his arm in self defense? Mai would shrink into herself as if it was not her but babu who had asked for the music to be lowered so that she would hear his threats and be on her guard before the arm was raised against her.

She had another similar habit. Always, before his bath babu asked for his shaving things and she remained so intent on her work that she could not hear him at all. She would not reply. He would ask again, and then with lowered eyes and a wounded voice she would say, 'There, on the stool.' The stool would be in the courtyard, near babu's bath water. (In the summer babu still liked to bathe outside sometimes, with the fresh water from the handpump). But she knew that babu took her to mean the stool in the bathroom. She would watch babu going towards the wrong stool from the corner of her eye, and seem intent on her work. A tiny shadow of satisfaction would touch the corner of her mouth for a second. Babu would say, in irritation, 'Where the devil is it, it is not here!' 'I told you, in the courtyard'—the same absent tone. 'Here,' I would shout out. Babu would walk on muttering and she would get up, pick up the shaving things and put them before him with a bang—'You don't listen...'

We were left wondering about this whole business. Mai kept fasts for babu, stayed up at nights making things for his guests, took care of all his needs, and then suddenly what happened to her? Was this any way to fight? Was this her revenge for not being able to speak up and fight? Why? What would happen to her at these times?

Our confusion deepened. Somehow we were never able to quite free ourselves of it. At every moment of 'giving', her memory appeared and warned—don't be a martyr. But at the time of 'taking', her memory made us feel guilty. We did not know what her fight was. And then we could not say what happened to our fight.

We kept coming home to take her out. It was she who tripped us over each time. We, our pity mixed with a little anger, would stand to one side and watch her.

We had grown up.

Just as Subodh had grown up before me, we had grown up before mai.

Outside the walls of the house was an old bazaar where we never bought anything. There were little shops for wood and iron, for *bindis* and ribbon, and green and pink plastic things. It had long become the market for the poor.

But this was the very place of our entrance gateway, on both sides of which babu had had round lamps placed. These stayed on for a while and then went out, because of the fluctuation in voltage in my native town. The electricity could go off if it rained too much, it would go off if the wind was too high, it would go off if there was not enough rain. Sometimes the two pale, round moons would keep shining as I noisily reached the gate in a rickshaw.

Once inside the gates there was no trace of the bazaar. A gravel pathway, a row of berry bushes, and the house glimpsed between thick fruit trees. It was whitewashed every Diwali.

Most of all we felt nostalgic for the food in our house—something we had earlier fought about the most. The memory would creep up suddenly and catch us by surprise, as in the game when someone covers your eyes from the back and asks you to guess who it is.

And then we were beginning to remember those trees where the *phakta* birds cried early in the morning, the road that hopping cranes crossed in the evening, the roof from which the swaying fields could be seen and the chugging of the distant pump heard, the same fields where we wandered looking for a blue jay and felt rewarded when we did. We remembered the palm trees with

the hanging nests of the *bayas*. We remembered the smell of
the *shisham* and *babul* flowers in the last days of winter and the
fragrance of the fine white flowers under the margosa trees. The
honey made of these flowers came to mind. Those dusky evenings
when the smell of burning leaves wafted around with the smoke.
The pattering of *neemoris* in the rains as they fell and a sweet,
warm smell arose. Nightingales, parrots, and a long, red, wild crow
used to come to eat green fruit on the lowering *neem* on the roof.
Sometimes the air was heavy with the smell of jackfruit flowers.
Sometimes subtle with *kadamb* smells. We would put the fresh
vinegar made from *jamun* in our dal, clean our teeth with fingers
smeared with salt and mustard oil paste. In summer, we'd pluck
okra from the okra fields and our fingers would itch for hours after
that. Dada would drink *sattu* flour mixed with water, and 'toast'
his hands before the coal stove. Dadi would make dirty jokes—the
English boy said to his father, *Pa, khana lag gaya hai* ('Pa, the food's
on the table,' or, 'I need to shit'). Babu's stomach aches after eating
barley rotis. Mai...mixed up in all our memories by being part of
every single thing in the house.

The house was old but solid. As our rickshaw pulled up
we could see babu sitting in an armchair on the verandah, mai
standing near him, waiting for us.

Babu would be pleased, and first make us sit down in the
drawing room.

Dada's sitting room had been converted into a drawing room.
His two pictures and sword in a leather sheath were still on the
wall. But around them were English landscapes framed by babu in
golden frames. Apart from the drawing room, there were pictures
on the wall only in the puja room. We had not developed a tradition
of hanging things on walls with a view to decorating the place.
The television was in the drawing room, the old sunken couch
with bent springs had new covers, the doors now had curtains and
the table had two copper storks standing next to the glass vase.

Babu had a screen partition put in dadi's verandah and a dining room was created. Now tables, chairs, plates and spoons were used. Subodh pleased babu further by bringing a china dinner and tea set straight from England.

Alongside the drawing room and dining room were mai's room, the puja room, the store room, endless rooms. The *khas* curtains had been replaced by electric coolers. The two of us, brother and sister, began to collect the small things of our past from all the rooms. We put them lovingly in our hostel rooms: the clay toys bought in the Diwali *mela*, the silk quilts embroidered by mai, the low stool woven in jute, little baskets for puffed and parched rice, a dish and cup made of engraved copper. I even took the brass pot. Subodh hung up dadi's embroidered zari shawl in his room in England and took the old bellmetal plates and bowls to give a proper Indian dinner there.

Babu had a new toilet and bathroom made where one could sit in long meditation according to one's new lifestyle of privacy! In front was a high window from which yellow *gulmohar* leaves descended in January like a fall of light.

Mai's memory somehow came to be associated even with that. Once while mai was bathing she called out to me to bring her the talcum powder. The door was not latched and I pushed it open a crack to put the powder inside. Mai was on the plastic stool drying herself. The leaves outside were falling like a rain of light. Her back was covered with drops and she was reaching back to rub her back with the towel. Very hard. On both sides of the deep line in the middle of her back.

I don't know why it was so strange to see mai's naked back. As if I could never have imagined that there was a back under her clothes!

That's how, one thing leading to another, we kept remembering the house—even when it was ages since we first left it.

Is childhood really divine, so that wherever it is, however it is, a temple is raised to it? We had believed the house to be a prison and felt it to be suffocating. Then we began to miss the very house as if there was some shadow there that would protect us. It was, as it were, the one place where no fear could remain unchallenged, with no ghost that could not be chased out.

In the house we had recognised the feeling of suffocation. In the open air that feeling was swept away and left nothing behind. What we could not feel any more we did not remember.

We had started to miss the house. Separately, Subodh on his own, I on my own.

Something had happened to me, only to me, after that first burst of excitement when I had left the house for the open outside. The longing to learn everything became moulded into a balance. I became more and more myself, separate even from Subodh, who himself became separate in his own life, who had even no physical resemblance to mai or dadi or bua or me. Fired with the desire to learn, I kept becoming free of values, of bonds. Fired by the wish to become something...

I was the bird poised in one place in the wide open sky that mai had shown...

I began to experience homesickness like a wave throwing me around.

When water dashed against our doorstep in the rains, washed the ground and swept back, my heart would beat fast. When the wind blew through the palm trees making black and white shadows my heart would call out 'mai!' One passing memory would join with another and there would be a chain of memories of the house. While putting dal in my mouth I would think of the raw mango that was put in mai's dal. We would pluck the raw mango bending down from the roof from the tree where the red-headed, black-and-white feathered woodpecker went tock-tock on winter mornings. We would stand still to watch him, at the same place where the spreading branches hid us as we inspected those passing in and out of the gate, and heard dada's roaring recitation and babu's timid echoes. There, standing together, we solved some puzzles, postponed some. I began to now think of the golden evenings at home and every memory had mai's shadow over it and me.

I kept writing to mai. There was nothing left to write about what I was doing, what I was learning. What I was doing was such that no one, no matter how well meaning, could have said, 'Oh, that's wonderful! So Sunaina is learning this, becoming that.'

'Well, you've made her great have you?' Babu challenged mai.

'She couldn't even finish her MA. She departed for a Fine Arts college without asking or telling anyone.'

When bua visited, she asked, 'Well, does one become a doctor by getting a Fine Arts degree?'

People asked, 'What is Sunaina doing?' The answer was, 'Painting.' 'Yes, yes,' they said, 'but what does she *do*?'

Subodh was in England.

Babu continued to send my fees. I kept painting my useless pictures in which corners of the house would get scattered and in the flow of the brush change from one thing to another. The spirits wandering around in the house, some of which had bodies, came to look alike. The canvas would have fleshy things. People would get confused whether I was showing one person or many.

Much later, when Judith came home and became familiar with the sights and smells there, she paused when she saw us both with mai.

We took her to our roof. She told me how she was able to locate my pictures now, in these extremely loving and intimate but closed surroundings. When she saw my figures, one or many as they might be, the heart melted but at the same time there was nausea. You felt charmed by the pictures but also revolted. She said that our home had come through in my colours, but that it had limited my vision. 'It may be okay for painting,' she laughed, 'but not for living...Get out of this suffocating intimacy or you will never be free.'

We had thought that we had already got out and it was only mai who was still stuck.

Judith and Subodh broke up.

Whenever we returned to the house we growled at mai in her chains. We now had our clairvoyant glasses on permanently. We could call her chains by their actual name. The desire to rescue her had made its way all the way to England where Subodh, studying on a scholarship, had been living for ages.

He asked me to come abroad. Babu asked mai—'Is this what she will keep doing, going here, going there?'

Babu panicked and tried to fix up my marriage.

But some things had been fixed for good already. When babu wanted to take me to see a prospective bridegroom, I refused. When he invited a family home, I refused to go before them. Mai pleaded with me—'What is the harm in going there? You can always say no if you don't like him. At least don't insult guests to the house.' I did go into the drawing room, but this young man, who was going to have a look at me, decide about the give and take with his parents, and then accept or reject me, was doomed in advance.

Babu started begging mai to do something. 'Are you mad? How will any marriage take place like this? If every mother worried like *this*, every daughter would remain unmarried.'

Mai did not say anything. It was always easy for her to fall silent.

It was always easy for me to start crying. I was both crying and smiling at myself—this marvellous person who lives alone, free, but is unable to pronounce a single confident statement!

'What, after all, do you want?' babu asked mai in dismay.

At this mai was not silent. 'Did you ever ask the children this question?' she said, and walked away.

I felt that I had done nothing at all, and what I had done was not worth boasting about, yet mai still believed in me...I could not have said why. But I could have borne anything armed with this belief of mai's. I stopped crying, but I was scared. Could I do it? Would I be able to do it? Could I prove that her faith in me was not mistaken? And what could I do, not for myself, but for *her*?

Mai was in fact afraid. She was not sure how solid the ground was under our feet. But not because the ground was simply unfamiliar and therefore seemed unsafe. Even then mai refused to say, 'Do this', 'Don't do that.'

Surely she would also have liked to see her children married, to have lights and *shehnai* music, to hear the sound of her children's children playing.

Surely she had been filled with hopes on seeing the lovely Nutan for Subodh. Nutan was the daughter of some acquaintance of babu's. We knew her from childhood. Babu's friend died. Nutan and her mother lived with Nutan's brother and sister-in-law.

That time mai showed me a letter. '...Dear aunty, my brother and sister-in-law are forcing me. Ma is unable to say anything. I am unable to refuse from fear of hurting her. I want to marry a boy in my class; he is a khatri and my brother says he will break his head if I do...And they are hiding from you the fact that I have white leprosy kind of marks on my back which have not been diagnosed...'

'Let's go,' said mai.

We crossed the bazaar and reached Nutan's place. Mai talked to her weeping mother—'Think carefully before you do anything. Today's children are not like us that they will stay put wherever they are asked to. If children become educated, it is harmful to force them. If your daughter is not willing to get married, you will make her life a hell by forcing her. At least see what the boy is like. Think of the caste later. The main thing is your daughter's happiness.'

And she scolded Nutan—'Get treated. Don't ever again try to achieve your aims by lowering yourself. This is the way of beggars, making you feel revolted by touching you with filthy hands and pleading and begging, so that you give in just to get rid of them. Don't ever stoop so low.'

This was the mai who, as a rule, did not speak.

It had been our complaint since childhood. 'Speak up mai. Fight back. Become what you want to be.' Being what she was, mai was actually nothing. She was a stooping, dumb, frightened shadow who moved only upon others' directions. We were full of pity. And were also somewhat put off.

It was someone else we could not forgive who had let this person become 'mai'. Because 'mai' was the synonym of 'not becoming'. Why was mai not permitted to become, to be real?

We would never be mai. We would never stay 'not made'. This was our profound belief, our bitter struggle, our life.

When a loose, old-fashioned sari with the end over the right shoulder appeared on an invisible body in my pictures, Judith again made a comment. That this person lost in this formless void is someone who did not 'become'. Who never got the right to 'be'. Who, if she exists, exists in her 'not being'. Her absence is her existence.

Judith advised me to name that picture 'Conflict'. But she wanted me to make, on that same canvas, another formless body that had a void for a face, but in the void appeared a faint shadow. Nothing need be too clear but there should be marks of a deep wound.

In childhood I got such a mark. The lights had suddenly gone in the middle of a thunderstorm. I thought of a trick to be played in the light of the candle and the lantern. I was in front, Subodh behind. I hid behind the door. By chance Subodh's shadow came before him, shivering in the gleam of lightning. I saw it and jumped forwards with a 'boo!' At that instant Subodh opened the wood-framed screen door, breaking my skull.

'It's symbolic,' said Judith.

When Judith came to our house she would stare at everything. She tasted, her mouth puckering, the sour beans hanging from the tamarind tree. She loved it when mai rolled rotis. She went and sat by babu when he did his *hawan*. She stared at Bhondu when he slapped and downed his tobacco. She asked hundreds of questions about the absence of toilet paper. Agreed, she said, that water is the best cleanser, but what do you do with the wetness of your body?

We were surprised that we had never thought of this nor had it ever occurred to us that water was dripping from us.

Judith stayed many days with us but she was not keen to look around in the town outside. It was we who sometimes pulled her to the river, or to someone's house, or to the old neighbourhoods.

The mango crop was spectacular that year and babu took everyone to Raghav kaka's village where, sitting in the orchard, a bucket in front in the style of dada, we had dozens of local mangoes cooled in water. Babu liked to eat his mangoes sliced round with a spoon to pick the meat, but local mangoes insist on being eaten the local way.

Babu was not displeased with Judith's visit as long as he could believe that it was Sunaina's English friend visiting. But Subodh could not care less—he took her around everywhere with abandon, disappeared with her on the roof, talked with her in her room late into the night, coming out only after everyone had fallen asleep.

Babu asked mai repeatedly, 'Have you asked? Find out. He is your son. These foreign girls. Yesterday she was smoking.'

Mai did not find out. She liked Judith's sociable personality. Judith wanted the board and rolling pin, 'I'll make the rotis.' Mai loved it. She made her all kinds of special dishes.

Mai took out the 'unbreakable' tea set from the box the day that Judith came. 'Make tomato and cucumber sandwiches, and rolls,' said babu. 'And listen. Keep the tea separate and milk and sugar separate. We will make it there.'

Hardeyi brought everything carefully to the drawing room. She had also been given a thousand instructions: stand like this, pick up the plates when the spoons are like this, serve from this side.

We were embarrassed. The hollow sound of forks and knives on those strange synthetic plates kept ringing in our ears. I tried to joke. 'Watch, Judith, this is the flat sound of your kind of crockery. When you eat in our metal plates you will hear music.'

Subodh gave us a talking-to later. 'What is this peculiar middle class habit? Kindly do not take out these new things while I am around. We will eat in what we eat in everyday. And the Indian food that is always made, not cutlets and what have you.'

Mai looked to babu who began to stammer, 'I never said...'— and mai looked down silently.

Babu wanted that mai should ask, find out. We wanted that mai should speak, speak out.

'Speak what? What do you mean?' asked mai. 'I don't have anything to say.'

'Come and sit down with us.' We explained, 'Talk starts by itself. She is interested in everything, ask her anything, what she does, how she does it, what is her life.' 'This is the great Indian approach,' we would comment, 'only eating all the time, eating and more eating, with no other interest in the guest.'

But mai kept busy in the kitchen. She did not speak. She did not find out. Maybe she did not even think. Only felt pleased when Judith came to her. When she felt, mai hugged her, put yogurt and sugar in her mouth and, circling her face with an *arti* lamp, handed her a sari.

Babu came to the station to see us off as always and sat down in our compartment to check out our fellow travellers. Like every other time he bore his eyes into them as if he would tear them open and reveal their intentions. When we protested he said, 'A girl is going alone. The world is full of bad people. One should be very careful.'

That day he told Judith, 'This is India. Trust no one.' Then he got after me. 'Where is the money Sunaina? Keep it carefully. Give it to Subodh. Is it in a safe place? Where is it? Tell me. Subodh, be careful. Stay together. Let no one get a hint where it is. Have you counted the luggage? How many items? Tell me. Don't get off at any station.'

At that time even babu's mumbling seemed louder than necessary.

Then Subodh became friends with Ritika. She also came home and babu sat around worrying. He was after mai, 'Find out. Ask. Tomorrow her mother and father will ask us in turn and what will we tell them? How is this affecting Sunaina? Think.'

But mai did not speak, either to him or to us.

Ritika did not laugh out loud like Judith. She was quiet and overcame her shyness slowly and at every step mai liked her. Mai always saw only what was before her, and formed opinions only on the basis of that. She did not try to unravel hidden layers.

Subodh was particularly annoyed at certain kinds of questions. When we were not around, babu would grab the opportunity and talk with Ritika about her caste, parents, family, occupation, and such things.

Subodh was furious—'What are you trying?' Babu tried to act casual, cleared his throat vaguely, then set out to find mai by herself.

We had risen above caste and so on, you see. Above tradition, caste, nation. We were not superstitious, not religious, not middle class. Else would we not also be samples to be studied on laboratory tables?

Our freedom was of the 'outside'. Even at home we were not of the inside and therefore were free. Abroad we were outsiders of course and did whatever we felt like. We were outside everywhere and alone. We wandered with complete freedom. Everyone else was dragged to our laboratory table.

Now I sometimes feel like taking a brush and making another painting. In which moves a body in a loose sari, whose face is invisible, not because there is nothing there, but because those watching her have blanks instead of eyes...

There was only a void where there should have been eyes. We took it to be the absence of the someone before us. We did have an occasional, sudden glimpse of someone, like a rustle in the breeze. But there could not have been anyone there! Who was it? If someone had indeed been there, why had she disappeared again?

That could shake us.

As did the appearance of Rajjo.

I was then still in the hostel. On returning from somewhere the chaukidar told me that my nana, my grandfather, had come to see me. I threw my head back and laughed. 'Whose nana? Whose message are you giving to whom, you idiot? I have no nana and never had.' But there was a letter. 'Daughter...my blessings...I am very keen to see Rajjo's daughter...I will come again...your nana.'

Rajjo? I didn't know any creature by that name. I wrote to mai. She replied, 'Don't go out for a few days so that your nana will not have to go away again without meeting you.'

When I saw the aged stranger my body and hands moved as if of their own volition and I bent down and touched his feet. He touched my shoulders and embraced me.

I had never given it a thought. Had mai had a life before us? Could she have been a little girl whose name was Rajjo? Could she have been something apart from us?

In this jungle of questions I suddenly found myself surrounded by silence. Instead of answers there was this wordless agony ready to swallow me.

Then nana took us somewhere. To someone in whose house there was a huge portrait of a sage who wore vermilion and sandalwood beads and on whom the light of the clay lamp cast swaying shadows.

Smiling, nana pushed me before this someone. 'Guess who this is?'

That person looked at me for two seconds unblinkingly and touched my cheek lightly. 'Rajjo's daughter? Clearly. The same face, only the clothes are modern.'

Subodh and I had gone for a walk. Through the lanes, up the hill, where the temple bells rang and the pink sky slowly disappeared into the night and got lost.

I was lost. I was Rajjo. Wandering in some forgotten lanes. Rediscovering my own forgotten people. In the old places, with the people that I had left behind somewhere.

And suddenly, it was as if someone had shaken me from a deep sleep—what if I had never left them? What if I had brought them here with me?

I cried out in fear. When Subodh told the beggar woman in front to get out, go away, as if maybe she too...in those old lanes that were mine...among those old people who were mine...had also been there...past...but not left behind?

I had gone home. I was wondering, if mai asks, what will I say and how will I say it? Mai did not ask. I told her, as if there was nothing easier in the world.

Then Subodh clenched his fists. He persuaded nana and had him phone mai. I was standing next to mai.

'I am Rajjo speaking...babu ji...'—a voice from thirty-five years back broke from within a bent-over old woman.

Both kept crying holding the phone.

The operator told them three minutes were over.

Mai had cried for the first time.

I was shocked because once again I had decided that whatever had happened in front of me was all that had ever transpired. That before me, apart from me, no one and nothing had existed.

But yes, I did see mai cry for the first time. I saw Rajjo cry in mai. And who was she but me, only in old-fashioned clothes?

Subodh arrived home with nana. God knows how a forty-year-old man and a twenty-year-old woman recognised the emaciated old man and the stooping old woman.

Babu was at a loss and sat around, embarrassed. The one who could have spilt sound and fury was dada but he was not around anymore. Dada was the one who did things. Babu was the one who let him do them and watched.

We stood to one side. We kept getting smaller, and smaller, and smaller still, and became invisible. We had given place to mai in our lives with ourselves right in the middle. Now we ourselves were nowhere. Mai was returning to the centre of her life, she was putting herself back from pieces to whole, and in her life there was no place for us.

No one saw us as we quietly went away to the roof, where we had spent so many days in childhood trying to find out things. From where we peeped into the sitting room to find out secrets. From where we had seen the person depart whose story we did not know and therefore we did not believe.

We had not known so we did not accept that right on that spot Rajjo had bid someone adieu... For what, for whom, why...?

When Subodh spoke I felt my ears had deceived me. 'How could she?'

Something was happening to him. 'There is no one so tyrannical,' he continued, 'and no one so helpless that he would let anything be done to him—no matter what—without protest. As if there was no option. No one can have such strength, no one can be such a weakling.'

Something was happening to me as well. I became more and more incapable of blaming mai, this mai who was inside me. How could I blame myself? How then live with myself?

There was that part of me that was the desire to suffer, that was mai. Religion had been left behind, custom and tradition had been discarded, but this thing inside me did not die. It held me against my will and I could only feel helpless at the very thought of removing it.

It was self torture made into a kind of worship. God, give this to him. Take this away from me. Destroy it.

Subodh got fainting fits in England. There were hundreds of tests without results. Judith came to me crying, 'I hope nothing happens to him.'

I had also asked that nothing happen to him. Punish me instead, but so that only I suffer.

Faced with this question of the life and death of another, I prayed to some unknown. Destroy my whole life but let nothing happen to him.

Judith came smiling, 'It turned out to be benign. There's nothing to be afraid of.'

It was mai who made me thus pray to remain submerged. Who made me an offender if I took something for myself. Who made me a martyr if I gave to others. And my whole fight was to not become either of these.

Nana had called mai. His relative's son was getting married. That is, mai's relative's son.

We got ready to go with mai but babu looked significantly at her.

Subodh began to shout. 'He is mai's father. Who are you after all to behave like this?'

Babu only said, 'Your mai understands. There will be others at the wedding. You children can't be told these things.'

I was watching mai. She was silent. She was not listening.

I knew, better than Subodh, that we would fail. How can you save someone who is determined to destroy herself? Someone who has decided that self-respect lies in letting the oppressor oppress and then making up herself whatever bit of oppression might remain?

We considered that self-respect lay in taking for oneself, maybe even grabbing for oneself!

She was a puppet whom we had seen dance to the tunes of so many. But even with so many pulling her she did not splinter into pieces. She remained whole. She continued to be pulled, but somehow kept her balance within her own control. Only, yes, her back got bent. All this was beyond us.

We became even more enraged—mai is lost somewhere else as well. We became even more determined to save her. And anxious to save ourselves from her. As if we had been appointed to this peculiar office and had to prove our worth even with our life.

Then Judith and Subodh broke up. The bundle of accusations she hurled at him included this one: 'You and your sister have only one aim in life—your mother.'

Subodh changed slowly. When it began I do not know. The beginning perhaps lay in that very relationship of us the saviours and mai the victim. Gradually, he lost patience. How can someone be saved who does not want to be? So, leave it. Why scream and shout? Why become frustrated? Let each one go their own way.

Mai had let us down often. She had weakened in the middle of battle again and again. She would be behind us while we were fighting. Suddenly we would see that she was standing with the enemy. We would lose our equilibrium: mai had changed sides.

A pained, feeble, oppressed thing who had emptied herself of all content. Who had made herself open and empty for everyone to fill with whatever they liked.

And they did fill her and this was totally unforgivable. Subodh would say with distaste, 'We have been fooled into seeing it as mother's love. We have turned a hollow thing into a goddess.'

We kept wanting that mai should fight to throw off all the different fires that everyone had tortured her with. But not to put the fire out. She should make a conflagration with the torches we gave. And thus become a complete person.

When the call came for Rajjo from a faraway telephone, Subodh said, stumped, 'How could she?'

We were sad that Rajjo had once gone away. But what really angered us was, how could Rajjo allow herself to go?

We were, ourselves, changed with our lust for life, ruthless in our longings and our hopes. We were the fighting generation and did not believe in any fight but our own kind. In truth, perhaps, did not count anyone as human but those like us. We could not see that there were others. 'Being' was us!

We had pride in the indefatigable strength of the individual, in the force of our youth. Even I, when everything around me had ceased to be so solid, was not afraid at all of my separateness and aloneness.

There was a slip-cover that we had been knitting since childhood. That had become so dear to us that we did not worry too much about the form we were fitting it on. We were busy pushing others around to protect that precious cover.

Which was very easy. It wasn't that there was one single mother or father whom we could get over-attached to, and begin taking their side. We had so many mothers and fathers! It was difficult to say which was our tongue, which our food, which our tradition. In this kind of situation it was easy to push everyone around.

We did the pushing around with a vengeance.

Including mai. The very person whom we wanted to save, the very person we wanted to see fight for herself, was the one we were turned off by, time and again.

But Subodh and I were also becoming different from each other, so gradually that it could not be discerned clearly. The fire in us was the same, childhood fire. But in it, separately, secretly, my own embers had started to smoulder. All by themselves.

Our 'we' was becoming hazy. Sometimes the 'we' would be 'both of us', sometimes only 'I' and then the 'we' became 'I' and 'he'.

Perhaps that followed from our sexes.

I also developed a disdain for mai. But with tears. With disappointment. While Subodh would move away with annoyance. He could not tolerate standing around helplessly.

I was weakening. There were chains within me and I was helpless: I could not break them. They might have broken me instead.

Subodh did not have to make any such calculation.

When mai once again quietly took the side of her enemy, Subodh was angry. 'The real fight has to be with you.'

Then he kept quiet and in the evening, when the three of us were in our room, he said to mai, 'Now I will do nothing more. You fight. By fighting on your behalf we have made you weaker. You speak for yourself.'

'I have nothing to say,' replied mai in her peaceful voice.

Her peacefulness produced a storm inside Subodh. 'You will have to speak,' he shouted out, disturbing the silence of the night.

That was perhaps the only time in my life that I exerted my right of being the older. The first time I thought of how she did not have to speak.

'Shut up, Subodh.'

Sometimes the first time is enough.

Everything went topsy turvy on that same roof where the mango branches bent lovingly over us as we hid behind their foliage and saw so much. Our childhood had been spent in the house and our struggle had been to escape the house. We had left the house and returned to it again and again. We were sitting in that same house surrounded by a peculiar suffocation and restlessness.

That was new. But old. Finished. But not past.

'She has made herself so feeble. The real fault is her own. The person who suffers oppression creates the oppressor. Let her go and fight her own battles now.'

'She has never ever fought so far...' I tried to defend her. From Subodh? I kept quiet.

'Nothing can be achieved here. Everything is rotten,' Subodh announced.

I looked at him confused and unsettled. His entrapment was mine as well. But...still...

'What are you thinking?' asked Subodh.

They were monsoon days and I remember the evening was the colour of fog. Where Hardeyi and Bhondu used to live at the back was a little pond. Thorny bushes and the wet ugly tops of branches were peeping from the top of the black water. A broken bench had fallen down next to the pond.

We had heard that Hardeyi and Bhondu's son had died. He had asthma. A faint memory existed of an infant with a bare pate, a dilated stomach and a runny nose. He had grown up only to have asthma and die so that we should hear of it but know nothing.

'I was thinking about Gopi.'

'Gopi?' Subodh said with a little irritation.

'That he was here and we did not know his story.'

'So?' Subodh shrugged his shoulders. 'We did not know a lot.'

I felt that there was a clue right here but what was it...?

'I feel confused.'

Subodh put his hand gently on my back. 'You should come there. Nothing can be achieved here.'

And seeing my solemn face he began to joke. 'This is the problem with you. You have confusion when you should have vision!'

Bua came during one of the holidays. She went with mai to the ladies' meetings in the club. But otherwise both were exactly the same—mai, bent over in spite of her belt and bua with the same refrain.

'When are you getting Sunaina married?' she saw me and asked mai.

Mai smiled and left the question alone.

I felt as if I was still in that place where I did not exist. I was being spoken about as an absent person would be.

I was immobilised a little by history, and a little by bua's sudden speech, and found I was awkwardly silent. But also resentful because girls do keep shyly silent when the subject of their marriage is broached.

We were plucking radishes and beets from the field. Bua's feet got caked in mud. What with her dusting her slippers and washing her feet, she forgot to pursue the matter.

But the moment stood still for me. The interval got stretched out and I was still planning some brave, crisp reply—'Should she decide or I?'...'Why are you asking her?'...'Ask *me*, I take my own decisions.'

Then bua asked me directly, 'What are you doing now?...What are your plans for the future?' The actual question echoed on top of these tiny innocent ones—'When will *that* take place? When will real life begin?'

Subodh was provoked. 'Future plans? What do you mean? She is already doing whatever she intends to do. Have you seen her paintings?'

Bua laughed, 'I will see the paintings when they decorate the walls of her home.'

Subodh's voice had warmed up dangerously. 'They are already decorating the walls of her home.'

'Huh,' bua said stubbornly, 'Neither this, nor there where she goes off to, is her home.'

I was getting ready to fight but stopped again.

Nothing was simple or natural anymore. If I argued it would seem a mere mechanical response. If I kept quiet I was being trampled under. In the 'what to do' the moment passed.

It was mai who could silence bibiji. 'Your homes don't stop being yours just like that! Why is this not her home?'

Again I felt as if I should be wearing a full-length veil in front of bua. When I crossed paths with her I would try to sneak past in case she began to ask me my plans again. Even others, like the sweepress, or Hardeyi, began to make me nervous. Following bua's example, they might now ask mai the same question in my absent presence.

But it did not bother mai. Her peaceful words were—'The most important thing is to stand on your feet. If in this day and age you accomplish that, then whatever will be, will surely be good.'

I complained about bua to Subodh. He gave me an affectionate pat and said, 'Don't bother, Suni. What do you need from them?'

Bua did not give up. She covered her mouth with her hand at the shamefulness of a nude woman in my sketchbook—'Dear God'.

Subodh could not contain himself. 'Bua, how would you understand what this is? You have taken as gospel truth the nonsense that someone once taught you.'

Bua did not like this. 'Yes, dear, now you can teach me right and wrong. All that remains is for us to wander around unclothed like cavemen. Then we might become cultured.'

They locked horns.

Subodh had taken up arms not for mai this time, but for me.

'If your goddesses are naked, you don't mind. Because they are goddesses you can't see it.' Subodh kept going. He meant the calendars that had Lakshmi, Saraswati, Durga in provocative poses, showing their bodies through tight, transparent clothes.

But bua's face turned ashen when Subodh said, 'You take the revenge of your mother-in-law's oppression on every young girl. You are an empty vessel making a rattling sound with whatever rubbish has been thrown inside.'

Mai scolded Subodh, 'Say what you have to say with civility.'

I kept looking from one to the other. Only looking.

I had asked mai, 'Bua is your friend, why don't you speak to her?' Mai told us about bua's mother-in-law, who had left her new home just a few days after bua's marriage and run away to her natal home. When her husband came to get her, she would not go and did not go. She did not disclose why. Her husband hung up a huge portrait of her in his room and worshipped it everyday. He took his son, that is phuphaji, to her, but she would not come and did not come. And still did not tell anyone why. The husband died leaving a sealed envelope addressed to his wife. In that he wrote to her to perform his first mortuary rites. So she did. Then she met bua and returned to her proper home. But never uttered a word. Only ruled over bua with a whip.

'Do your trampled dreams give you the liberty to do or say just anything?'

'No.'

'What is the point of understanding everything if you won't act on it?'

Mai said, 'If I have to understand I must understand every point of view. If I understand every point of view it becomes difficult to act.'

I was impatient looking at the defeat on her face. But also by seeing the victory on Subodh's. I was tired of victories and defeats.

If I was on the side of victory I became an oppressor; if I was on the side of defeat I became a martyr.

I could only look from one to the other.

One day bua came back from an outing somewhere. She said, 'Come, I want to talk with you.' Taking me to one side she began. 'Listen, I know you are very attached to mai. If you take a careless step, what will happen to her?'

I understood with a pang that the news of Ahsan had reached home somehow.

'Girls should be friends only with girls. Don't you remember that Nita...?'

I remembered Nita. Bua had made fun of me in childhood. 'Right. I have seen these friendships between girls. I'll ask you when you grow up where that precious friendship went that was never going to break. Why are you not with her with whom you said you were going to spend your whole life?'

'...you can tell me...' bua was saying.

'I have nothing to tell.'

'...she is your mother, if she asks me, what will I say?'

And at this challenge all my self-respect stood up angrily in its full height. 'My mai will never ask you and if I want to tell her something I will not need to go through you.'

As I made my dignified exit babu was caught standing in a worried pose at the door.

'Aha! So that's it.' I gave him a piercing glance and went straight to mai. I was going to express my anger and instead burst into tears.

Mai became serious. 'You *know* that I never set anyone to find out anything.' She went to where bua and babu were sitting thoughtfully.

'Will you trust the whole world first, and then your own near and dear ones?'

She gathered up some cups and plates and left.

I watched immobile. This unshakeable faith that nothing could shake and nothing would shake. Either Ahsan does not exist or if he does, he cannot be bad.

When Subodh came home I did not feel like telling him anything. He might get mad at anyone.

But bua had touched a chord somewhere. The atmosphere became electrified. I had grown up and there was no Nita, there was Ahsan, and according to bua there should have been Nita.

I observed mai quietly. Had Rajjo had a girlfriend?

And it became clear that there was a secret rule behind this, which made dadi's, bua's, mai's, mine, everyone's girlfriend get left behind somewhere. Behind dadi's grand poses and bua's harshness and mai's peacefulness and my modern conflicts was a great silence that had swallowed up those ruled by one-sided laws...where Rajjo had disappeared...

Babu was happy that Subodh was in England and that I had also been there. But he was getting overwhelmed by us. He did not really know how to fight. Dada was not around to wrap up every thing with a roar of his voice. And mai was fooled into believing any old thing we ever told her. Judith came and he saw cigarette smoke. That was proof. Subodh's temper was further proof. My painting was testimony to the same. All around there was evidence of her naivety.

He became totally desperate when he heard about Ahsan. He kept telling mai, 'Don't support the children in these wrong things. Do something.' We kept telling mai, 'You give babu support by keeping quiet. Do something. *Fight.*'

There was much we ourselves could not say to her and we had never asked. Priyvadan Samant had greeted mai in the club in front of us and said, 'How are you Mrs Tiwari? I saw Mr Tiwari from afar that day in Lucknow with someone. I thought it was you and went closer, but it must have been a relative of yours.'

Mai said with equilibrium, 'No, we have no relatives there.'

Sometimes Subodh and I rode past that house on the scooter. We did not see mai's hand-knitted sweater again.

We did not stop telling mai to come with us. Even to England. Periodically, Subodh got furious. 'Forget it, we will never ask you again.' Then later, again, a ticket, a programme, a book. Again, pleading.

But what was it that was happening to me? I did not like anyone's arguments. Even Subodh's. If he lost I wished he would win; if he won I wished he would lose.

Babu was unable to say anything to us and instead kept telling mai, 'You are so ignorant that you believe anything. You are like a round eggplant rolling around on a plate.'

But it was mai and not him who knew that when Judith was there we had had a punch party on the roof. He did not even know that mai allowed us to cook fish and chicken in the kitchen, giving Hardeyi time off, on condition that we would clean up the pots and pans ourselves and not touch the oil or spices with meat-soiled hands. Babu continued to consider her the ignorant one, in our clutches. He believed that we could make her do anything we liked.

If we told mai anything, she never said no. What she did is another matter.

She kept quiet. Even babu was sick of this now. He was convinced that by refusing to see or hear, she was encouraging us in our wrong ways.

Babu went after her, 'Find out, who is this Ahsan?'

Mai said many things at first. 'It must be someone who works with her. She must be meeting so many people. Everyone can't be of the same background.'

When babu went on and on she was quiet. She kept busy doing her work, then would leave and go somewhere else, without a word, to do something else.

I showed mai my picture of Ahsan standing on the colourful mountains of Ladakh. 'He is a sculptor mai. He makes statues. He is at our institute.'

Babu still kept asking, 'After all we must know who he is, what he does, how he knows her, a Muslim after all...'

Babu was wilting so much with his worrying that when Subodh said, 'I don't want to come here anymore,' I thought, 'Just as well.' It was seeing us before him that made babu's worries come particularly to life.

Babu's hobnobbing with swamis and sadhus increased partly because of these worries. The chaukidar would come running with his torch, 'Augarh baba has arrived.' Mai would give the keys, the gate would be opened and Baba with his one, two, three, or whatever number of jelly-fleshed disciples would enter without hesitation. 'We will stay here tonight. We will tell babu a solution to his problems.'

Mai would be labouring away so that nothing was lacking in the service of the guests.

We would keep smouldering. I had also begun to speak up but it was Subodh who had inherited dada's voice. 'Give whatever there is,' he would roar. 'Why are you busy making new things? Tell babu to send Bhondu to the restaurant for something. What is this?'

Mai would shush him. 'We will certainly give what we have...I am just making a little more vegetable, it looks as if might run short. It doesn't happen everyday...speak softly please...'

Babu entered once at this point. 'I did not ask for this. Yes, do send Bhondu for kachoris and vegetables. Here is the money.'

Mai turned to us, 'Go please. You're not doing your own work and you're disturbing me in mine. When we have food at home why should we get restaurant food for a guest? Now leave me alone for ten minutes.'

Subodh ground his teeth, 'Let us go Suni, nothing will change here.'

Mai said softly as we left, 'Doesn't it hurt to make Bhondu run around all the time?'

I was left speechless. I felt as if really nothing could be done. To give to one was to take from another. We were all losers, all caught in a web—babu, mai, the two of us...Bhondu... No one could win.

Our innocent childhood memories, our hopes, our beliefs, everything was being clouded over by a kind of frustration. The house was full of suffocation in all its corners—dada's, dadi's, babu's, bua's, mai's. Hardeyi's, ours... Behind the yellowing pictures, under the new striped covers of the old couch, around the holes in the Kashmiri carpet, in the grill on the ventilators... It could pour out of its hiding place at any point to make us gasp for breath...to overflow from our eyes.

We had grown up and could not stay a 'we' any longer. We could come together on the same side but we also realised that we had our separate truths. We realised that the soundlessness that surrounded the vast terrain of pleasure and pain, bondage and freedom of everyday life may be the same in principle but was a different experience for each person. It had a certain colour for me, for us women, which it did not for Subodh or for babu. Indeed I was afraid of it because it stretched forth from before my birth. That silence had become mine from before there was me.

The past is that god—or devil—whom we cannot worship but who is present everywhere, surrounding us inside and out, holding us in its clutches. We are merely a miniscule part of it. We are helpless.

I was helpless from my childhood. Helpless in my desperation to save mai, helpless in not being able to save her, and then helpless before our frustration and that resounding silence that was our history, mine, and Subodh's, separately.

Subodh believed that we had successfully punctured that silence and become free. He was happy to see my self-sufficiency—I lived alone, drove a car, painted. I had gone to England and it had been like a homecoming. Subodh wanted me to come there to stay. When it was past sunset in this big city of our big land and it became necessary to escort a girlfriend back to her place, he would say, 'Suni, we have none of these problems there. You can go out anytime at night, sit anywhere in a cafe, meet anyone. One is *mobile.*'

He was after me to come to England. We would have an exhibition of my paintings. Something would work out. There was so much *scope*. And *here*, half the time here goes in preparations, half in covering tracks. What is left for work?

Babu's face was lined with wrinkles. Where is Subodh taking Sunaina now? If she goes there who will be left to be saved from ruin?

Mai still did not voice disapproval. Life keeps carving its own paths. Let it. Let them.

We were after her saying, 'Mai, *you* come too. Subodh has a home there—wouldn't you like to see it?' Babu had however made it clear without saying as much that one doesn't spend thousands of rupees without cause. Subodh had gone to study, and that was different.

When the rationale for my going had been agreed upon, babu's wrinkles became deeper and deeper but he couldn't say 'no' even to himself. Subodh had dizzy spells, someone from home should be with him for his care, so Sunaina should be the one to go.

'Yes, that's right,' he would say, 'who is with him? Someone from home should be there.' 'But there's nothing to worry about,' he'd say again, 'I too have dizzy spells if it gets too hot, but we should ask the doctor anyway.' 'But we should not get involved with a doctor,' he'd say yet again. 'The doctor has to earn his living so he'll certainly say there's an illness and make someone perfectly normal into an invalid. Subodh should come home and mai will make him all right. Bring him back with you. There's no one to give him good food there.' And then finally he'd say, 'Write to him to come home, there's no need to go at all.'

But those times when he could have stopped me from going were gone for good. He came to see me off at the airport. Mai sent *besan laddus*. And a letter: 'Write all the news quickly. Health is everything. If you find the kind of sweater you got for Bhondu in a sale, get two or three, it pleases everyone because they are foreign. My blessings...'

Babu kept saying his beads in the next—'Turiyatit baba... baba...baba...' He panicked when he saw that travelling with me would be labourers going to the Middle East, unemployed and in search of jobs. '...baba baba... there are no restrictions even on planes. God...' He told the passport control, 'my daughter is going. Alone. Please ask one of your officers to take care.' I flashed a pitying smile and shrugged my shoulders helplessly. I felt I should hurry up and disappear inside before I too began to see wolves everywhere.

Before going inside I forced babu to go to the airport restaurant and ordered two glasses of orange juice. Babu drank it up but scolded me as well. 'Why are you so restless? Think of baba, peacefully.' When he got up he told the waiter that the tea had been slightly sour and had not even been hot!

That was my first time on an aeroplane. It took me no time at all to become an excited little girl again. But how nice it would have been if, instead of the sheikh next to me, I could have had mai. I would talk to her about everything I saw. Look down here, the ocean on this side, the ocean on that. Strange, isn't it, we on top of the clouds, and the sun playing below? The clouds as solid as if they had been the earth? There is Dubai, here the West Asian desert, Jordan, Kuwait, look, the whole atlas spread out! The snow on the mountains below is covering them like a white sheet. Then the sea again, Istanbul, the Black Sea, Bulgaria, Yugoslavia, Lintz—mai, the horrible Hitler's country—Germany, Alps—look at the greenery—London. Taste a little, I would say, this is champagne, just a little. We would fly together.

I have had dreams like this from childhood that keep circling like clouds and enter the house through doors and windows. Some even burst into rain.

Childhood was past and dreams were clouds gathering and dispersing, and mai was a burden that we had been carrying around, sometimes advancing carefully, sometimes stopping when tired, sometimes wishing to put down the bundle in despair, unable to do any of the things easily.

Mai waited for us with babu at the house. We kept going back, sometimes alone, sometimes together. The house was peaceful with babu's guests visiting, bringing their wives along. They would be delighted to meet us because we had set foot on the hallowed land of England. Subodh was definitely a hero but I was no less a heroine. For my English, my travels, my freedom, and because all these were mine and not their own daughters'.

We came again and again. Because mai would be lonely. Babu stayed out the whole day. How could the fields and wells make up for the company of humans?

It was sometime during those days that Vikram came home with me. He was at work on a field survey in a nearby village. Subodh was not there but I invited Vikram home. Babu might still have tried to say that Subodh's friend had come on work, but Heinz was also working on the same project and staying in some guest house in the city. He came to pick up Vikram every morning and I went along too some days.

Babu could find no excuse for Vikram staying with us. He told mai that when both the boys were working together why did they *both* not stay in the same guest house?

I crackled like lightning—'Can my friends not stay here?'

Babu's tongue ran away with him—'Peeeople...people do not like it...you should not call a man...a fr...a friend.' And finding himself inadequate to the delicate demands of the situation he whined to mai—'You should tell her. The children are old enough to understand the difference between right and wrong now.'

And he sneaked away without meeting anyone's eyes.

Mai did not say anything. She would give Vikram his dinner with affection. She threw away his torn bag quietly and made another one exactly like that of strong denim with a zipper and everything. When Vikram was leaving he asked me for a glass of water and as soon as I turned around he bent to touch mai's feet.

Vikram left and babu kept ranting and raving, repeating to mai, 'It is getting difficult to even go out now. People keep asking all kinds of questions. At least they should not go out together in this town.'

He avoided me and left mai's side when he saw me. If he didn't see me he would look around carefully and reach mai. 'I hope you've told them. I hope you have forbidden them.' Just then I would appear and he would suddenly tell mai in a loud voice, 'Stitch the button my shirt.'

We had always been concerned about this—this habit of putting mai in front to say and do everything. I would follow mai around so that she could not find herself alone with babu. If I left home I would keep worrying about what was happening there and what babu was doing to mai, and how mai would never tell.

Alas. That I could save mai. Our wish was so stubborn that we could not imagine that there was something unattainable about it. Or that some extraordinary steps might be needed to attain it.

'Leave, mai,' I kept saying, 'Subodh is calling. At least you can go to visit. Babu too if he feels like it.'

But since when does life follow anyone's directions? It leaves familiar paths and turns to new ones all by itself.

Babu went to Lucknow on work sometimes. He went once with some people and just as they entered our town on their way back a truck ploughed into their car. Babu and his three companions were thrown afar. It was dark and no one discovered them till morning. When they did, it was found that two had already passed away and babu still breathed but while his breathing was more or less normal, everything else in him was twisted and broken.

We rushed home and just on that day when we were not up to meeting anyone, bumped into some childhood friend of Subodh's—Arif or Zamir or Jiwan, something like that. He had studied with him in Sunny Side Convent. He was a businessman in Bengal and met Subodh occasionally when he came home.

We were suffering. He was in a hilarious mood. Since we did not want to talk about ourselves and had on a mask of normality, we had to tolerate his banter.

'Do you remember...,' he was recounting memory after memory. 'The carefreeness of those days when we came to the station for fun? Stood around on the platform drinking tea? And remember when so-and-so mail would come, we would dash inside in a crowd and grab the seats, thrilled that the up-down people thought there was no seat, peeping and moving on to other compartments? The whistle would blow and we'd jump off, guffawing that a whole compartment was going completely empty. Remember...?'

He went on and on. Subodh sat hiding behind an unnatural smile.

I was on my own because I did not know him much. I was safe and was beginning to wonder, were Subodh's and my childhoods separate as well?

But we had come back together as 'we', aghast at life's unpredictability. So aghast that we reached the edge of suspicion: where in fact faith begins—can everything happen without a reason? Can life indeed be so fearful, chaotic, meaningless, random?

We had thought that the age-old rusted doorway had begun to creak upon, and found that suddenly new, strong stakes had planted themselves all around mai. And she was imprisoned again.

Mai dropped everything and got busy picking out the glass pieces from babu's tangled hair.

Babu's body was broken. He was covered with plaster all over, but his head remained irretrievably bent to one side, his shoulder protruded on the other, and his waist was crooked forever. His feet would not fall straight. Babu dragged his broken body from one spot to another, made some noises with an unsteady tongue and did everything with mai's hands—bathing, dressing, eating.

Mai was trapped—holding the forefinger of this 'child' of hers to make him walk.

A new cry of despair escaped from us. How very trapped she was! Worrying, we would drop our work, take time off, keep coming back home.

A shadow wandered around in the busy house. It had done so right from the beginning. Now there was a gloomy pall all over, all the time, of utter failure. As well as that shadow...

Babu also became a shadow.

It was in those days that 'she' came. She did not have mai's hand-knitted sweater on but something clicked in us and we recognised her. Even though her body never juggled with loose fat under her clothes.

Mai kept sitting, close to babu on his bed, changing the bandage on his forehead. The strange woman sat nearby on a chair, the head of her umbrella sticking out of a coloured plastic bag.

I remember a few things clearly. She was coughing repeatedly as if she had an ordinary cold, and after each cough said, 'excuse me.' The cough arose in her throat and, even if it did not come out, the 'excuse me' came out. She was like the girls educated in English medium schools who, as they grow up, cover their knees carefully with their frocks, join their legs, straighten their backs, make their hankies into balls in their hands on their laps, and at everything move slightly and say 'Sorry', 'Thank you', 'Pardon', 'Excuse me'.

The wind was fierce and mai told me to close the window. I got up and went. The trees and plants outside were beating their limbs, as it were, in agony. I thought of my institute, behind which the sea must be going mad.

When I saw the gulmohar leaves falling, I saw in my mind's eye mai's back, before it had become so bent, which I had seen shining with water drops and in the middle of which fell a long, shiny, shadowy split, like a branch.

I stopped, lost between these various thoughts. Babu was lying behind me broken, 'that' woman was sitting there and to close the window I was having to hold the curtain again and again. Which was getting work out and was flapping madly like the trees and plants and seas, as if it thought it was also a part of nature.

That woman spoke, whether to mai or babu I do not remember. I had a kind of premonition. I looked at mai and saw on her face a dawn-like peace and then a golden contentment.

Up on the roof Subodh was depressed. Mai had to suffer so much.

I cast my gaze full of confusion on him. He was unravelling the tangles of gender and society and tradition—mai who was bent over, mai who stooped, if it had been mai and not babu who had become bedridden, would everything have changed the way it had in the house?

Now it became even more difficult to leave mai to herself. We became even more anxious in our desire to save her.

Subodh had to go back to England. He made me fill in this and that form and took them with him.

In the meantime I returned to the house, bringing all my painting paraphernalia with me, with instructions to Vikram to keep coming there, on some work or the other, or even without any.

Babu's eyes seemed to glint with a drop at the edges. 'Aa... baa...' he stammered unclearly to mai.

Mai came to my room—now she slept in babu's room—and sat down without a word.

When I asked her what it was, she said that if possible, the two of us, Vikram and I, should not stay together here as we did.

She left. There was a cold weakness in my veins in the place of blood. I could not leave mai and go. And if I asked Vikram to stop coming...?

I realised with a shock that mai for the first time in my life had asked me for something, and then, too, not quite asked, just...

Judith had argued with us that she held us in her grip and if we did not fight loose, we could not grow. She was the one who had imprisoned us, not babu, not dada, not dadi. 'You will not grow. You will not become anything. You will drown in this swamp of sticky intimate belonging.'

It was not as if mai told me to get married, or else leave him. How much did she understand?

When Vikram came the atmosphere was unbearable. I would wait for him to leave. I tried to avoid being alone with him because even then it seemed we were not alone.

On my canvases floated new images, in extremely closed rooms, watched by two silent eyes or a quiet shadow or a speechless fluttering sari end. The eyes open in the middle of a void. The shadow standing on one side of a wall. The sari end tied to the arms of a chair. As if these were peeping in from behind, responsible for making each scene a 'private' one and for it not being private either.

Vikram left. But that strange woman began to visit.

And mai spoke no more to babu in that feeble, dying, pitiful voice. Her tone had a force, her hands a business, every movement had a purpose, her eyes had confidence. If she saw babu do something wrong she raised her voice slightly and directed—'Oh, oh, what are you doing? Sit down...no, do not bend over, sit down right there, immediately...someone else will pick it up...*sit.*'

Mai was my guide—for what I must *not* be.
Mai was trapped. She remained trapped.

Babu's illness quietly swallowed up the little spot of contempt that had entered us and all we could feel was an infinite sadness well up inside. In spite of that woman. Or maybe because of her.

We had not learnt to ask questions. We just stood quietly on one side, casting a pitying look at mai.

We felt pity for babu too but the truth is that babu was only an expansion of mai for us. If he existed at all. He was tied up with her.

And mai, in our sight, was tied up with us. In spite of everything that we had seen.

There is a trap formed by words, indeed one formed only by thoughts, in fact one formed merely by the tiniest doubt. The person thus entrapped sees everything only in a certain colour, even things of quite a different colour.

Our sight had been sharpening since childhood. The faint tick-tock of some unfamiliar clock was audible but as if our ears were deceiving us. Some unseen flutter did reach us, but we considered it an illusion. If we saw some unfamiliar glimpse of mai we blinked our eyes in surprise and then re-drew our old familiar image.

Or one can say that regardless of what we saw or heard, we knew only this—that mai was captive, sad, and helpless. And we—we were born to save her.

But while lying on the roof with our eyes closed and repeating our old ideas, if we opened our eyes, the bright sky would fill our insides and something sharp would pierce us, something dangerously like questions.

It could be that the truth is so vast and so tangled that, unnerved by this, we would prefer to take some small, shrunken fiction as true only because of its simplicity.

And it is also that a trait or characteristic can be recognised in a relative stranger, but on knowing the person better it gets mixed up with many other traits in him and becomes unrecognisable. If that person who nana introduced me to had seen me everyday, maybe he would not have said—'Oh, is this...Rajjo's daughter...?'

We are so hesitant before vastness, before its unknown waves...

But why should we not fear the unknown? We can go ahead because we *know*, otherwise would we not be immobile in one spot? It is life's own condition that you imagine you know and keep moving. That moving on is then called life.

We understood later that it is not only we who moved. Life itself moves on, at its own speed. The speed is the same for the person standing still in the storm and for him moving along on his own. It is not we who are moving life along. Or that life stops moving for the person who has stood still.

We saw mai standing at one point, and made her stop still there forever.

Like the visitors to the house who, in spite of the passage of many years, fixed me forever in some familiar moment of my childhood. For them I was the one from somewhere back then. Faltering before their eyes, I would myself put on that cloak of childhood. My dimensions may have been an adult's but I would pull myself into becoming small again and perform accordingly. I felt sometimes that I was living a lie in that house. I would panic. Run away, let the lie not be known.

But I could not leave mai in the clutches of that house and go away. I stayed on. Subodh wanted to have an exhibition of my paintings in England. He was confident that the foreign audience would be impressed by the subjectivity of an Indian woman and love my paintings. He was hopeful of a terrific success.

But how was all this to come about? Mai could not be left to her fate. Subodh could not return. I could not stay there forever.

Mai mentioned my work. 'Does a freelancer not need a college or institute?' I should think of my career; everything would go on as usual in the house. Then she left the room hurriedly as she heard the tapping of babu's cane.

Babu no longer left the house to go anywhere. The scooter stood covered in tarpaulin awaiting Subodh's return. Babu would keep reading. Until some visitor arrived. Or he would call mai. She would keep sitting near him.

I rarely went to babu. Subodh at least could talk about things. Such as how the Asians settled in England were experiencing ill will against them. And so on...

I could not think of anything to talk about. The status of painting in our house was dirt, so it was not a subject for conversation. I also found it difficult to follow babu's speech after his accident and felt embarrassed to keep asking again and again, 'What?' 'Tell me again?' 'I didn't get it?'

I could neither stay nor leave. If I went I came back very quickly. If Subodh left he immediately started planning to come back.

In fact the house had become home again, for better or for worse. And we were getting stuck in the peculiar subterranean mixture of security, safety, and suffocation.

It also happens that one can be saved from taking a decision. Things decide themselves. Many people are constitutionally like that. Whatever happens is the best according to them and they quietly abide by it.

We were so restless. Mai was trapped, I was trapped, what was to be done? There, once again, in that very house.

Life gradually fell into a regular pace. Babu was confined inside the house, but comfortable. Mai looked after him as if there had been something lacking in her care before. Once I was helping mai set out dinner, and was taking the trolley towards babu's bed. Babu stretched a hand towards the fruit bowl nearby and mai said, 'No, no, don't eat that, dinner is served.'

Babu had already unpeeled a banana. He stopped and looked uncertainly from the fruit bowl to the banana. Then asked mai in his unclear way, 'May I...eat...this...?'

A child asking a stern teacher.

Mai removed the banana from his hands. 'Have your dinner, then eat it.'

Days passed. I would stretch out my canvas on the roof in winter and paint. It was nice there with childhood memories—our gravel path to the gate on which a snake could easily be spotted, where the cobwebs from the ventilators to the walls glistened like silk threads, where the monkeys had fled but the peacocks still came and dropped their feathers.

I made many pictures in the house. But, I began to think helplessly, was life to be spent there?

No, we were not pleased. Then, babu had a stroke. Such a stroke that anyone could see he had not long to live. Subodh came rushing, babu met his eyes once, and went into a coma.

Mai stood nearby. As did the doctor and we, and Hardeyi and Bhondu. Babu was restless. He was in pain, and his emotions were restless too. We were standing still, our hands clasped in front of us, like statues. As if we were death and babu was life.

So many shadows from the house's past came and stood around us.

Then babu opened his eyes just once and raised them through the maze of the glucose drips and the oxygen pipes. Seeing our dead eyes he deliberately closed his own again.

Then he stayed in a coma, as long as he stayed alive.

We were not saying it, avoiding each other's eyes while recognising the same thought in the other. Babu was going, mai's last bond was breaking...

We were sad. We were not saying it. He may have been a stranger but he was our father after all.

Some hope that had been born in our childhood and been suppressed, that had grown with us, and had blossomed into a longing, now came and stood at the point of consummation. Maybe for a moment our heartbeats speeded up secretly. But then our eyes overflowed with sorrow for babu.

But mai was at peace. We had almost never seen her cry. She was busy with babu's work. There was an end to her gourmet cooking, her sewing, her knitting, her gardening, her ladies' meetings.

She will be able to do all this, and much more that she will learn...the words emerged from Subodh through puffs of cigarette smoke.

We had been adamant from the beginning that we would not leave mai to be mai. Our experience, our deep thinking, our weighty analyses had taught us that mai was a hollow thing because this society had made her hollow for its own advantage. We would supply the human content, give it the opportunity to grow so that this suffering, this oppressed hollowness of centuries would slip away and mai, now mai no longer, would become her full self, a not-mai.

The not-mai was the human for us.

The doctor told mai to look after her health and take her vitamins. If she did not take care how would she look after others? We were also worried about her health. But mai, crooked, bent, feeble, became restless as soon as she lay down. She would get up and apply herself swiftly to something.

When I think of those day, I keep seeing mai combing babu's hair with a lustrous smile.

It was from the roof that I had seen the bamboo at the back grow tall and show beautiful blossoms. I broke off long branches laden with flowers and was arranging them in a copper vase in mai and babu's room. Mai told me, 'When the bamboo blossoms, it means its days are over.'

Babu left us.

He was with us one moment, gone the next.

The house was full of bua, phupha, people. Mai made ample arrangements. Bua burst into tears—'Bhabhi! Put a pillow under his head, that ice must be so cold!'

Mai only said—'Bibiji!'

And the rest of the dialogue came rolling from our childhood— 'Why are you talking such nonsense?'

We did not feel that anything had changed at home because mai's quietness was the same as before. We felt that everything was the same as always. It is now we realise two simple things—first, everything ran according to rules at home because its manager was mai. And second, because of our overwhelming love for her, we never did bother with what was behind her silence.

Bua always wanted to come and be with her brother but she could make it only in phuphaji's vacations. Now that her brother was not around, phupha chose to drop all objections and bua all but made our house her home. Or maybe as she grew older, she also became freer to gradually retreat into her childhood.

Bua was living with us. Even when she went home she came back quickly.

'Now look here,' she would tell mai and try to take over some of the work, 'I have a "plan" about everything that needs to be done, so don't try to interfere.'

Maybe mai would be cleaning up babu's papers in his room.

She had sent a packet to that woman, which, from its shape, looked like neither a packet of papers, nor a parcel of clothes.

Our house was like the earth itself, independent of an individual going or coming, revolving according to its rules. The seasons kept revolving. The things to eat, the things from the fields and orchards, kept changing.

Hardeyi still helped out in the kitchen but Bhondu only lay on his cot outside his room and coughed ceaselessly.

A sizeable contingent of serving people had come to express their sorrow to mai. The sweeper from the road, a carpenter, the postman. The same people came at the festivals and mai gave out sugar, grain, cloth, and cash at odd times as appropriate to the zamindari style of our house.

Subodh and I were at home, still waiting for the right moment.

I don't remember the exact occasion but it was raining and a bird sat on the branch opposite, its wings puffed up, its neck deep in its body. An odd drop from among the ever dripping rain would strike a leaf in such a way that it shook all by itself with a wet of shine. The bird would suddenly swipe at it and it was as if the whole tree with all its leaves shivered.

'It's essential for a man to be around,' bua stated in her most stubborn voice.

Mai was cleaning out dal and the two of us were busy with something.

But how could Subodh come back and if he could, what would he do here?

Subodh said something that made bua for some reason turn to me with a sneer, 'Huh! She has lived in England for two days and now wears it as a badge and wanders around as if she doesn't belong here?'

I said quite softly, 'What's the matter, bua? I'm right here.'

'Right here indeed. There's no sense in your being here.'

I did not want to remain silent when I heard this accusation about my girlhood. So I said, 'Why not? I have a right to be here, and mai and I can manage just fine without a man.'

This made the argument go in undesirable directions.

Subodh tried to restore equilibrium. 'If they want to. But we have no intention of staying on here.'

Bua got provoked. 'What do you mean? Do you want to turn this place into an abandoned ruin?' Then she added worriedly, 'if you can't leave England and you can't leave your mai, then let Sunaina be the one to do something here.'

Bua and phupha wanted a school to be opened in part of the house. Many had chosen this course to save themselves from the threat of the Land Ceiling Act. This way we children could save our ancestral home. Subodh could be the Principal. If he didn't agree then I could do it. After all, I wasn't doing anything else.

'Why should she stay here bua?' Subodh insisted. 'She has her own work.'

'Painting can be done here as well,' bua said stubbornly.

Mai took the dal inside and bua said, 'Think of mai.'

'We do exactly that,' said Subodh.

'By leaving her alone?' asked bua.

'Certainly not.'

'Then Sunaina...'

'Certainly not.'

Bua looked at us expectantly waiting for a bombshell.

'Mai and we...' Subodh had started when he saw mai coming and stopped. Stopped speaking before that very person, mai, for whom we had been waiting to do what we had to do, what we had grown up to do, what we had nourished inside us like a vow.

Subodh looked down with embarrassment. I said to bua, 'You can run a school here.'

'What do I have here?' said bua, her voice heavy with embarrassment as well.

We were merely passing time. We were the ones, rather than mai, who could not leave the house. We were the sorrowing ones. We were the ones gathering up our courage now that we were almost at our goal, as if now...now...it must happen...

Phupha also came sometimes. He came by car with his sons, and as before we set out, only now without babu, to go to various places.

There was a railway crossing in our town. We needed to cross it to go everywhere and as soon as we left home one of us was sure to say, 'Oh! I hope the gate is not closed.'

In our childhood we would suddenly hold out an arm or a leg before the other—'The gate is closed—the chuk-chuk train is going.'

This time we found the railway crossing closed and the line of cars, trucks and rickshaws getting longer and longer.

The gate was closed for ages. There was the sound of a train, a light visible from afar, and smoke. Then a little mouse of an engine passed the tracks in front of us, going chuk chuk chuk and whistling happily.

Mai began to laugh. I remember her laughing. She kept on and on. Her whole self was laughing, her eyes were watering, she had to stuff her sari end into her mouth, and we looked at her, smiling and a little surprised.

She explained sheepishly, 'We were waiting for so long, thinking a long grand train will pass, and what had stalled us was this'—pointing to where the engine had passed—'this little pipsqueak.'

We smiled, somewhat condescendingly. We did not laugh. Nor could we accept that her laughter arose from amusement. It was an unnatural laughter, according to us, after babu's death. We held that she could not laugh any more those days. She had laughed only that one time, the very lonely, very unhappy mai.

Whom we must not allow to continue living there any more...

We realised later that we had simply not understood what was happening. Then even later we realised that we had actually understood something even while deciding that we had not, but there was so much more that eluded us then, and later, and now. We used our eyes, for instance, to see only the shadow, when there was a whole figure we should have seen that cast that very shadow. We used our ears only to hear the silence when there were many, many sounds to hear.

And then there came the time when the silences swallowed us up and there was nothing to see, nothing to hear.

It's difficult to say how much time passed. If one opens up the papers of the house's sale one could remember the dates.

The mustard plants caught a disease. Mai had the whole crop cut down. There was no other way out.

The grass was mowed and all around was the smell of fresh-cut grass.

The winter clothes were being aired in the courtyard before being locked up in trunks again.

In the same courtyard the washed grains of wheat spread out on charpoys to dry were being steadily eaten by squirrels.

That was where we had drawn the lines with chalk to play hopscotch. But earlier. Earlier.

Mai's chalk-white sari gleamed next to Hardeyi's old cotton one.

'When' has no meaning, in fact. It was a time that became part of every moment of our lives forever.

A breathless atmosphere, a quiet house, the same habitual routine, when we were going to say the heretofore unsaid to each other, and I went to mai with a cup of tea.

The cup of tea fell from my hand. Her hand fell from Subodh's grasp.

'Mai,' I screamed, 'Mai, babu has left us.'

That was long past of course.

'Suni,' said Subodh in shock, 'Mai has left us.'

The bamboo flowers were still blossoming in the pot.

We kept standing there. We did not feel anything. We forgot to grieve. Just stood there. And looked at the ashes that had fallen from mai's eyes in a pile in her lap...

Mai left only those ashes.
And us.

We saved the ashes away from others' sight, only for us. We kept them private, between us on our roof, and kept looking at them with uncomprehending eyes.

This is where it all was, all that we did not understand and could not understand, which was not part of us, which was apart, which was something beyond us.

Someone beyond us.

Recognition of whom we had erased in our pursuit of recognising ourselves.

And now we were in agony.

The house became a ruin. No one was left to look after that huge ancestral house and that farming and garden. We had of course broken our ties with it long ago. Whatever was left was broken for us by mai, by her betrayal at the crucial moment.

She had let us down constantly.

We had become two from being one for quite some time. Now we split up even further, into many different 'I's'. One might talk cleverly with the lawyer, *vakil* uncle, about the property. The other might get entangled ghost-like with the cobwebs in the ventilators.

There was talk of selling the house. Bua was prepared to take the other shares together with her own. Wills were being read and pondered. Paintings, carpets, spittoons, jars, all kinds of things were being packed up.

Overhead spread a vast, overcast sky. Down below was a silent darkness.

We would forget to walk one moment, to stand still the next.

Very strange things came to mind. Seeing the karonda pickles in a jar, to scold that I had not been told how to make them. Or take down a photograph to look at it as if for the first time—mai and babu on a scooter, the husband laughing, the wife smiling shyly, looking at each other.

When? When? One would get dizzy wondering. Mai smiling at babu? Why? What did they have between them? Where were we? Were we not between them?

What had happened to the house? It had suddenly started whispering. Look at this. It was right here but have you seen it?

The taste of the food changed. The smell of the house changed.

The place, symbol of our frustration, was calling out to us sadly. Its call was creating a turmoil inside us. Our past was spread out on all sides in that house. It stared back at us, sometimes with dry, sunken eyes, sometimes with soft, loving ones. The stare of these helpless, imploring eyes tortured us.

The house was weighed down by this torture, this sadness. And right in the middle of it, like sparklers, was scattered our laughter. If our oppressed childhood had been spent there, so too had our joyous childhood. How could oppression ever be complete? If we had seemed to be silenced from the outside, was it that all the waves inside had been stopped as well? Our voices rising in song in the middle of this oppression had nothing repressed about them at all.

Pitilessly, Diwali came that year as well. Mai used to make camphor *kajal* in a little clay pot. Bua did the Lakshmi puja and lit one single lamp to put on the doorstep to allow all the ancestors of the house, from many generations past, to enter comfortably.

We, standing on the dark roof above, saw them enter the house. From up there in the dark, we listened to their mystery-filled narratives.

Bua and phupha tried one last time. 'We'll take charge of Sunaina. We must fix up her marriage somewhere.'

Subodh stayed calm.

No one had the right any longer to take charge of me.

Many days must have passed. But not too many because vakil uncle was still coming and the talk about the house was going on.

Everything was going on without letting up.

Flowers were everywhere. It must have been February. The breeze would bring leaves fluttering down. If we sat in the sun during the day we would feel hot. If we sat inside we felt like wearing socks.

Hardeyi was cooking. The fields had spinach, beetroot, beans, carrots, peas, cabbage, everything. The jackfruit tree had baby jackfruit. The bottlebrush was blooming. Mai would put those flowers in the vase in the sitting room and *champa* and *mogra* flowers in a heap on a platter. Guavas were weighing down trees. The vendor regularly brought around fresh green peas for us.

It got dark early. Subodh and I went to bed early too. The warmth of the quilts was lovely. Lying in them we would listen to the noise of the city. It was the time for weddings. Tuneless bands kept playing late into the night. The whistle of the train sounded in the morning, then the restless sound of wheels on the bridge.

Evenings brought a strange feeling. Vakil uncle wore very thick glasses and from a particular angle, the pupils of his eyes would become like two stones staring from each side of his nose.

The air had sharp, cold bristles. We closed the windows and curtains and huddled. We could see vakil uncle depart from there—he in front and the chaukidar behind shining a strong torch on his legs. Which made his trousers transparent and the outlines of his legs become red and fuzzy stripes like the burning elements of a heater.

We were depressed. It seemed that nothing would work out. It seemed as if we were neither there nor anywhere else. It seemed as if the whole revolt had fizzled out. We felt that death could hardly know itself, only life really knew death. That mai did not know at all, only we knew. And we also felt that it was useless to try to break and mend everything around; why did we not peacefully accept things?

Subodh, lying on one side, would say something and his voice seemed to be coming from a faraway, closed cave. As if he was speaking with his mouth on a clay pot.

Subodh happened to break a pot around that time. Hardeyi was bringing water. Subodh jumped up to take it from her hands when there was a loud noise and the pot splintered.

Subodh and Hardeyi picked up the pieces and wiped the floor for a long time, and Subodh kept apologising ceaselessly, 'I am sorry. How clumsy. Sorry. I am sorry. I don't know how I dropped it. Sorry.'

Hardeyi was struck dumb with this unimaginable civility on his part.

I was annoyed. 'It's all right,' I repeated many times. Subodh, looking helpless, kept on—'Oh, how clumsy, I am sorry.'

There had been a telegram. 'Sorry about Rajjo. May God rest her soul in peace.'

There had also been a telegram from Kashmir addressed to me from Subhan Mian, who found out god knows how. He was nothing to me; Ahsan and I had stayed in his houseboat once. The telegram smelt of the wood of the boat. The night we stayed there, there had been a storm on Dal Lake and the houseboat seemed to be breaking up. It's our last night, I'd told Ahsan. But we survived and Subhan Mian arrived early in the morning with tea. The houseboat had a foreign name and Subhan Mian fondly arranged German, French, Russian, and English magazines of odd years on the lounge table.

Bua was busy looking after mai's house. We were wandering around like two shadows in the house, ready to take the things of our childhood away in boxes. Suddenly, on the way, we would hesitate when we found the cool ashes from mai's eyes lying somewhere. In odd rooms, on odd things. As if she was saying, look, turn around and look. We would look around startled, with wide eyes and find mai coming towards us in strange forms, now laughing, now speaking, now hiding a blue bruise under a long-sleeved jumper, now with babu but not in the way we had seen them together, now Rajjo...and also crying, but not for us, not for anything known to us, but for something or someone we did not know.

We were running after mai for so long and now that it was absolutely too late, we found that our key, so to speak, did not fit that lock at all that we wanted to open to find mai. Our hands were empty after all.

We stood on the roof looking towards the gate as we had been doing since childhood. There was a strange new feeling. That mai had stood there, so many times, alone, looking at those coming and going through the gate, thinking something to herself. What?

But that was wrong. Completely wrong. Mai never came there. Even at Diwali it was we alone with Hardeyi and Bhondu who lit the lamps here. Why this feeling?

Then I had another feeling. Mai had stood in the very spot where I was standing now. But I had never seen her. This had happened before my time, because mai was mai before me, and even before that, and we had never ever accepted that.

This was a new agony.

Rather, this was mai in agony within me.

This feeling of mai within me would not leave me in peace. The ashes lying here and there gave rise to so many narratives, which all remained incomplete, became dust and flew off. Who was mai after all? The mai that we kept 'saving'? That we wanted to take away?

When we tried to fill her up with things of ours, what precisely had we removed from within her?

We had again been let down just as we were perhaps on the verge of understanding. How, now, to begin to live with her again in a way that we could see her as what she was, and not as we preferred her to be? A mai on her own, not a mai moulded by babu or dada, or a mai moulded by us. A mai suffused with her own breath.

We had set out to hold mai down. Childhood passed, or maybe did not pass, but a later time did dawn. Mai made our minds into sieves and escaped through them again and again. We stretched out a hand to get her but instead found ourselves holding some end of ourselves.

We had seen her parda. We saw the parda as a lifeless thing in others' hands, pulled here, pushed there. We thought that this was mai, this was mai herself. We did not sense the dignity behind the parda. We made this being who did parda colourless and lifeless.

We had felt suffocated at home. We had wanted to get out, to get mai out. Subodh did escape. Mai left. And I got suspended somewhere in the middle.

I suddenly stopped in the middle of gathering up our childhood things with the intention of carrying them away abroad. Mai had given me this carved silver key bunch saying, 'You like old designs, have a locket and earrings made of this.' Dadi had used it for her keys, tucked into her waist. Mai's face swam before me. I closed my eyes but the face did not reappear. I stopped.

'I don't want to take any of these things.'

Subodh also stopped.

'I don't want to go anywhere.'

His face paled. He looked strangely behind me as if there was someone coming stealthily towards us.

'Have you gone mad?'

But now we were able to make our decisions separately. We were already used to it.

Subodh all but wept. 'Mai has left us, Sunaina. Babu and dada have all gone. The house has gone.'

He began to shake me. 'Mai is no longer with us, Suni, mai is no more.'

We were both crying.

I did not argue. Mai had gone, the house was gone. But ashes were scattered around and a soul had lived and blossomed in their coolness. My selfhood lay somewhere in these ashes.

Subodh could not take it any more. 'Suni, leave all this or nothing will be possible. You can do nothing in this prison.'

It was easy for him. He did not have to pull at his own self, break and disfigure himself, to become free from the prison.

'You don't have to fall into the same bonds as mai. You are young and I am with you.'

He grew angry. 'Don't become sentimental. There were some good reasons why you left in the first place.'

I was unable to explain the feelings in me. I want to live, Subodh, and live more. But I came alive, my last little pore came alive *here*. I cried and screamed in this prison. Every bit of my body was ready to fight here.

There in that little corner I was free, but in the wide world around I am dead. I do not want to be dead.

'You will not last here. You cannot live in this place. Suni, Suni'—and his loud voice echoed against the walls—'You will never be anything here.'

'Then I will be nothing,' I said in my stubbornness. Although I had not meant to say any such thing.

And Subodh roared like a wild creature—'Yes, be nothing, just like mai, don't be a real person of your own.'

Wrong. Wrong. I was not able to explain. Mai had not been nothing. It was we who had made her like that. I did not want to be mai. I would not ever become mai in any case. Mai never did want to make me like her. Even if I wanted to, I could not be mai. I can shrug mai off. I do not like sacrifice because that was mai's burden. I will not be like her, giving and giving and pretend this giving is my taking. I do not want to make martyrdom my goal like her and make sweetness and timidity my habits. I have to fight her history, reject her being, and do that by taking and taking, and only then give. Give only after taking. I have to fight till then, fight her herself, the mai who is alive, who is in me, who is in the fire, in the ashes, who is there forever. Before whom I bow. I will fight her.

Subodh was desperate. 'Fine. Suffer.'

Mai suffered. She pulled her fire inside. But do you understand, mai had a fire too; she was not hollow, she had a fire? We had seen her suffer only for others but did not see her suffering from her own fire.

Yes. I will suffer. I will pull and pull mai's fire outside and keep it alight.

And do so here. Right here.

Because freedom is not the air blowing around in a cramped corner. And a prison is not only the clearly outlined bars in the window.

I was not able to explain to Subodh that there was only smoke billowing inside and outside me. That this was the reality, this smoke, inside and outside me, full of countless relationships in their sweetness and decay, whose sweetness made me breathe in deeply, whose suffocation made me breathe out fast. That I was trapped in this smoke, choking, breathing. This was the smoke of the unseen fire, of mai's fire, of the fire from before her, of the fire of today, and of... Smoke, and also embers that were still alight and shedding ashes. In the surrounding greyness there was a head, and a trunk, that I had thrown away by mistake, that I had to find, with my life or my death, find somehow, sometime, and put the head and trunk together.

In my childhood mai had put down a ladder to get me out of the pit. I would keep climbing that ladder until I reached...

We left peacefully. Both of us left the house. I brought only one thing from the house. That piece of paper from the picture frame that was crumbling, changing into a cool silvery dust. And the ash was inside me, becoming warm, and smouldering gradually again with the fire of mai's unlived and unseen life...

AFTERWORD

Mai: A Discussion

Part I

The Matter of the Mother

M*ai*, as the title suggests, has at its heart a mother.
The mother is a familiar one. I have one like that at home right now, as I type. She is sitting next to me, bent over. She will not rest against the cushion because of her inbuilt grid of self-sacrifice. We just had tea. While I was looking at a paper, she carried the tea tray back to the kitchen and sneakily washed the cups and spoons, although that is my job. She will offer anything there is in the house: food, drink, place to sit, newspaper to read, TV channel to watch, window to look out of, bathroom to visit, and so on, endlessly, to all of us while denying that she needs any of this for herself. She does not merely say this in a hundred ways, she enacts it consistently, in subtle, hidden ways, until we are all pawns in her game of supreme self-sacrifice. Like the mother in the novel, while appearing weak, she has the strongest will of us all: we may question and dither, but she knows what she wants. She may seem to change her mind or veer from one position to another, but the consistent calculation under all of them is the good of others. Especially her children and their families. Nor have her sons with all their good intentions succeeded in making her aware of her rights. The more they have tried, the more they have failed. She continues to keep her fasts, worry about others, sacrifice all comforts, be bent over rather than straight...

So what *is* a *mother*?

It is not that either the author's text, or this discussion, has an answer to that question. It is that we are both interested in the question. My reading of the text, and my reading of my mother-at-home above, suggests that a mother is, at the most elementary level, both weakness and power, innocence and manipulation, self-denial and self-interest. It is the paradoxical reciprocity of the two that creates a version of the master–slave dialectic, which leads to confusion on the part of observers, and miscalculation by both 'oppressors' and 'reformers'. *Mai* goes to the heart of the paradox.

Anthropologists, sociologists, scholars of religion and history, all academics with an interest in the constructedness of gender roles, have their perspectives, and give answers to this question. It would be outside the agenda of this discussion to survey the literature in detail but we could note the constructions very briefly. First we have the earliest, most realist, economistic studies according to which there are two clear-cut sexes, of them, woman's is the oppressed one, and this remains stable across time and place. There are numerous inflections in this approach, such as those that question the effect of development, of multinational production and trade, and of modernist ideology. The most sophisticated is certainly the Marxist one, such as used by Claudia von Werlhof. She writes:

> The 'true essence', so to speak, of this division and its starting point is nothing more than women's natural monopoly: their child-bearing capacity. In no mode of production throughout history is the child-bearing capacity, the prerequisite of production of humans, so central as in the present... It is no accident that capitalism's so-called 'Population Law' is considered to be nothing less than the 'general law of capitalist accumulation' (Marx). It is this law which turns women into child-bearing machines and is responsible for the so-called population 'explosion' (1988: 178).

In this view women have developed 'a specifically feminine capacity for work' because 'they *had* to develop it' (von Werlhof 1988: 178). Everything that women do, however, and the way they do it, is for the benefit of 'the system':

> The friendliness, submissiveness, being-always-at-others'-disposal, healing-all-wounds, being-sexually-usable; the-putting-everything-again-in-order, the sense of responsibility and self-sacrifice, frugality and unpretentiousness, the renunciation in favour of others, the putting-up-with and helping-out-in-all-matters, withdrawing-oneself and being-invisible and always-there, the passive being-available and the active 'pulling-the-cart-out-of-the-mud'—the endurance and discipline of a soldier (179).

On this super-capacity rests the whole system of capitalist accumulation. One might extend the same terminology to add, of feudal exploitation as well. It is a hair-curlingly accurate picture of Rajjo, the mother. This is what the mother I have at home is.

In a second approach to mothers, the data base is not, as in the above, international statistics of how many hours women work versus the wages earned, illuminated by insights into their subservient behaviour. The data is 'ideas' about women, in literature, mythology, sculpture, painting, rituals, and politics. These 'images' of women, it is argued, shape the 'reality' of women's lives (Jain and Mahan 1996). And though some correspondence between the two can be empirically discerned, there is just as often contradiction, and no particular technique is used to demonstrate either relationship except of informed hypothesis and elegant statement. Ideas or images of women—of South Asian women, for instance—as in Tulsidas, regional literatures, Bankimchandra, Tagore, Gandhi, and so on, can therefore be notoriously contradictory and also predictable. The mother, particularly, is imaged in the following ways: (i) as a deity in Harappan civilisation, the putative origins of the Mother Goddess in South Asia; (ii) as *shakti* or embodied power, by Shakta sects and practitioners of Tantra; (iii) as a parent who can be either (a) benign, as one would find in biographical and apocryphal literature, or (b) violent, as Hindu mythology cheerfully informs us; (iv) as the nation by later 19th-century nationalists, particularly Bengali; and finally (v) as invisible and voiceless, according to recent scholarship.

The third approach to the mother would be one that would turn over the preoccupations of the second approach above, by first casting doubt on the relevance of the data through a theory of reading, and then on the conclusions that use androcentric models in good faith and with naivety. This perspective would question models, concepts, language itself, 'redefine the important questions, re-examine all previous theories, and be critical in our acceptance of what constitutes factual material' (Dube 1986: xvii).

Mai hints at using many, or all, of these perspectives in turn, but none of them exclusively or consistently. It plays a kind of trick on the reader. It leads the reader from holding one view with full conviction to moving around to the other side and viewing its reverse. Each time that a watertight case is made for the motherhood, mothering, and mother's destiny of her whom, for lack of any other name in the book but mai, we will call Rajjo, the author turns around her correct politics and questions this status.

But, somehow, with the peculiar genius of literature, *Mai* also gives us a character who encompasses at least two faces—maybe three—without the negative implications of inconsistency. She opens up for us a past of girlhood and freedom, then a present of bondage and servitude, then a future yet unknown but full of potential.

Mai shifts the question from 'What is a mother?' to 'What kind of a person is this mother?' Rajjo is behind a parda, but, as the novel gradually suggests, it is a curtain that provides serenity and privacy, and contains behind it a bustling world and life. This world goes back somewhere into the past, before she was a mother, before even she was a wife. In this hidden world she had—she *has*, because the text keeps her 'fire' alive (or, if I may be allowed a witticism, as my computer informs me daily, '"Word" is saving "mai"')—a selfhood, smiles and laughter, loves and losses. A selfhood is a fire that smoulders. It can be turned inside, as Rajjo does, and becomes invisible because it is behind a permanent curtain. Or it can be turned outside, as the daughter Sunaina does, when it sets fire to the curtain itself and becomes visible, maybe engulfs some territory involuntarily. That no one at all is privy to Rajjo's selfhood makes her all the stronger. The fire smoulders as strongly, none the weaker for being contained.

This, one may argue, is not necessarily an emancipatory vision. Sunaina's fire, turned outside, does not immediately seem to explicitly illuminate anything or lead her anywhere. She is, at the end, consumed by frustration, her mind filled by fog. Rajjo's fire might give her an inner peace, but outwardly she is broken. Like 'the woman who walked through doors' she has her own satisfactions and life of the mind, but she cannot claim that she was free to make her choices. Others do build up walls around her, close doors, erect barriers, 'oppress' and 'maltreat'. Rajjo is praised by her mother-in-law, but oftener abused by her husband, for her very silence. Does Rajjo's case suggest that all mothers and wives who are only dutiful and silent, are supremely fulfilled? What about the argument that

> a woman's heart has secrets that even the funeral pyre
> cannot reveal. Suppressed continually by the opposing
> forces of religion, society, even destiny, they finally

> explode within her. Like weeping without tears, living
> without breathing, like a mountain of fire that cannot give
> out smoke, they are contained inside her and shatter her
> inner being (Antharjanam 1998: 45).

A fire is a difficult metaphor. Unlike the narrator in *Mai*, we do
in fact associate it more with explosion and consumption and a
final reduction to ashes than with a quiet containment behind a
curtain—that most combustible of things.

Or, in a more universalist vein, the argument can be put thus:

> Is this enough? Is it to live?... Does virtue lie in abnegation
> of self? I do not believe it... Each human being has his share
> of rights. I suspect it would conduce to the happiness and
> welfare of all, if each knew his allotment, and held to it
> as tenaciously as the martyr to his creed. Queer thoughts
> these, that surge in my mind: are they right thoughts? I am
> not certain (Jacobus 1986: 41).

For those who think these thoughts, such as Sunaina, the question
is a live one, and finally a confusing and unanswerable one. So the
question, 'Is this mother's life enough?' is not answered, either by
the author, or by the narrator, or by the protagonists. For me what
the book suggests is the bigger question: *Whose question is this?*

My mother-at-home's, ma's, case should tell me. (I would give
her a name too, because to merely name people 'mai' and 'ma' is
to deny them their lives beyond their roles of mothering—and yet
I feel constrained by the Indian idea that you do not call elders by
their names. So I cannot call *my* ma by her name but I can call 'mai'
Rajjo. I am an insider to the former and an outsider to the latter. An
insider is one who can respect out of conviction, that is, who can
accommodate the irrational within the rational. An outsider is one
who strives to be purely rational). The one thing I knew best about

ma was that 'she was a very good student and always stood first in class.' Then I knew also her practices: how she held her son's chin as she combed his hair, what she fed her sons and daughters, how she cooked spinach. Who told me all this about her? Her children, exactly those who wanted to make her into something. When she speaks to me, it is *never* about herself. She will never say, I was a good student. Or even, this is what *I* consider a good breakfast and what I gave my children. Her talk is always about her children, and, to her credit, about me.

Does *she* have a mountain of fire within her? Does *she* have the question if her life is 'enough'?

It would be going against the grain of all my empirical knowledge about her to say 'yes'.

Ma, and mai, may both simply exemplify a familiar, annoying characteristic of mothers. They will never say what they want. They will outguess you at the daily level and put you before themselves. They will refuse to assign themselves preferences, tastes and choices. They retreat from accepting subjecthood. They will not to the end admit even whether they were the ones who ever decided or not, and then, having travelled a certain path, were fulfilled or not. Did they, do they, ask the question or not?

We will not know.

A mother like Rajjo seems precisely the dissolution of the subject.

But perhaps a dissolution of the subject is only what *our* limited vision suggests?

Vivekananda's response to a question regarding how he would help widows, was, 'Am I a widow? What is the logic of asking me? Do not widows have the intelligence and the will to themselves decide how they would be helped?' What *Mai*, the novel, like Vivekananda, does is raise a very large discussion on the question of 'the subject' and its desirability. And a related questioning of the viability of the project itself, when the problematisation and the solution both come from others. Are the subjects here the questioners, or is the subject Vivekananda, or are the subjects the widows? Obviously it is not the widows, and Vivekananda refuses to take up the mantle, so it is the questioners. But why is Vivekananda's simple point so difficult to keep in mind in scholarship, even feminist scholarship? Why is silence taken for absence? Why, in the imagery of the novel, is a curtain short-sightedly, unimaginatively misunderstood to be not only a barrier, but a barrier behind which there is *nothing*?

Rajjo has done more with fire than simply turned hers inside for herself. She has tended someone else's, allowed it to grow, even arranged the curtain in such a way as to allow its flapping to incite the flames. Sunaina is free because of her mother—free to use what she likes of the past and discard the rest. She does not even realise perhaps, by the end of the book, how free she is. But we feel, we suspect that she will go on ever onwards, and still hold on to her past as bestowed to her by mai.

Mai can speak eloquently when necessary and can be adamant and persuasive through other means when she wants to be. She *chooses*, however, most of the time, to be silent. Even when there is no speech, the assumption that speechlessness is not a choice is unjustified. *Mai* demonstrates, again and again, that silence is a weapon. It can be used to aid or to hinder. It can purposefully make the other angry or enthused. It can stand for approval or disapproval. It can indicate resistance as much as complicity. Rajjo, like the mother I know, and the women I have studied (Kumar 1994), is a master at silence. A silence does not indicate non-communication or un-readability. The potential here is analogous to that of translation, where a text is not untranslatable because it has not been translated, but is simply, as it were, awaiting its ideal translator (Benjamin 1985).

Mai is certainly the posing of an intellectual's question, an author's and a reader's. It is an intellectual's discovery, as the narrator, of herself, including her widening comprehension of her mother and her relationship to her mother. *Mai* is not the mother's voice. As a novel, it is meta-fiction, on how a novel may be written in search for the mother's voice.

But as a translation of the mother's silence, it gives a wonderful insight into how silences can be pursued. Here, the daughter has enough at stake, in rootedness and pain, to keep pursuing her mother's mystery. Apparently, in intellectual endeavour, there is far less motivation. But what if there was to be that passion for the unspoken, or that instinct that tells that after all everything is not spoken in words?

Perhaps the clue lies partly in the difference between the brother, Subodh, and the sister, Sunaina. He is a scholar of sorts, apart from being a man, and relies, one supposes, both professionally and personally, more on words. Sunaina is a painter, apart from being a woman, and seems to trust images that are incomplete, suggestions of movement, shadows and clouds.

What the novel *Mai* suggests to us, I submit, is that the method should follow the subject. We do not know 'what' mothers are, we do not know if a given mother is 'fulfilled' in what she does, or what else she 'wants'. But we could progressively know whether to ask certain questions, how to ask some others, what any of them might imply, how to refrain from asking and retrack, how to pause and begin to comprehend little glimpses better. We could start evaluating silence differently than how our dichotomous, rationalist world, much like Subodh and Sunaina's, tells us to. We could question agency, strength, and weakness anew. We could take the plurality of each of these things seriously. *Mai* is partly about a mother, and largely about the methodology (a social science term that the novelist, I suspect, would not like) of asking about mothers.

~

There are at least three other mothers in *Mai* apart from Rajjo: the grandmother, dadi; the servant, Hardeyi; and the aunt, bua. Dadi is laughable. She adores her son so much that it blinds her to any possible shortcomings in him or virtues in others. She is a terrible mother-in-law because she is such a devoted mother.

Hardeyi is a failure in a very precise way because her son dies, the implication being that it is because of her poverty and ignorance. She is *destined*, and through her, her son, to be lost to history. But she shows solidarity with other mothers, and women generally, by routinely cooperating in Rajjo and Sunaina's efforts to live lives maximally ordered by themselves.

Bua does not have her children around her. She interferes, unsuccessfully, in her nephew and niece's life. Her voice is shrugged off by them as irritating, but is also internalised, at least by Sunaina, as the prototypical voice of the Order that is trying to make her into a puppet. This is also a mother. A mother who speaks for patriarchy and the non-freedom of women.

No comparisons are made or suggested. But *Mai*, like life itself, poses the conundrum that the problem of the mother is created, most volubly and aggressively, by mothers themselves: for Rajjo and Sunaina by dadi and bua.

Mai plays this other trick as well, then. It shows us a range of mothers. But it calls only one of them 'mother'. It calls itself by that title, that is, makes itself the story of this *one* mother. This is a trick played not only by this novel but by all fiction and real life itself, or rather, by our ability to read fiction and to read real life. We can analytically see in the book that all mothers are not alike (such as Rajjo and dadi) just as all non-mothers are not alike (such as dada and babu). We can see the same in innumerable variety all around us in real life. Yet we forget that, both every day in our own lives and while we read *Mai*. Popular consciousness has it that mothers are nurturing and sacrificing. A hasty report on or version of *Mai* could be that it is the tale of Rajjo as the archetypical mother, not dadi, or bua.

But though she is nurturing and sacrificing, there is nothing archetypical about Rajjo's versions of these processes. She nurtures her children towards questioning and independence. She sacrifices with conflict-free self-confidence. The results of these processes is the surprise. As an archetypical mother she would have glorified these very virtues. But her children condemn them and her daughter will not 'be like her'. She can produce change, that is, through her own preferred tactics, and do it so effectively that we are not quite aware how it occurs.

Equally significant are the non-mothers in the story. Dada is the foremost, repressing all the women for his own pleasures, confirming fear in the heart of his son to keep him subservient. He is a monarch who does not have to bow before anyone—opposite in this sense to dadi, who, monarch as she is in her own way, is ready to wash the soles of her son's feet.

Then there is babu, supremely tangential to his children's socialisation and upbringing, to an extent that in spite of his rare feeble efforts, he does not win them over to even a basic empathy with him. Only in relation to the domineering habits of his father does he seem mildly attractive, or perhaps tolerable. Otherwise, throughout, he is the weakling, who cannot eat heartily like his parents, take care of his own clothes, puja, or other needs, and cannot speak his mind directly to his son and daughter. He seems capable only of commanding his wife, albeit in a feeble or indirect way. But this non-mother presents his worst side in the non-nurturing, non-befriending, non-supportive, and non-socialising role he plays with regard to his children. He is their enemy. We can almost see how this damages him as it does them, and how it weakens their relationship. He is merely a victim of a certain structure of parenting that is understood to be the norm. He seems to have the inclination for more gentleness and love than he himself or others expect of him and give him a chance to easily display. Thus, denying and being denied his androgynous possibilities, babu suffers from being distanced from his children, not achieving either the excessive masculinity of dada nor an individually formulated sense of self worth.

Last, there is Sunaina herself, the narrator. Unmarried and unattached in any stable relationship to the end of the story, she is determined to be *not* like her mother, presumably including in the central characteristic of maternity. She, together with Subodh (also a non-parent), is chided often by her mother for not understanding, not letting her alone, for kicking down her house of sand, as it were. The suggestion is partly that Sunaina is immature, that she lacks some insight that comes from Rajjo's involvement with the complexities of childrearing, from the protection that only mothers can give to children from cohorts and seniors out to destroy them.

Yet, of these second generation non-mothers, if I may be excused for the awkwardness of the phrase, Sunaina stands closer to the mother-heroine. Why? Is it because, of the two non-mothers, she is the daughter? Therefore she bears the mantle of her mother's legacy, some connecting thread that does not snap however much pressure it has to bear, of reform, reason, rationality? What is the perception Sunaina has of her mother's, grandmother's, and other female forebears' shadows upon her, their beings mingling with hers? Are we back to the argument that there is a sisterhood of women, that one is biologically programmed towards certain traits and characteristics from being born a woman?

Even Rajjo seems to share this profound belief. Her mother-in-law is her harshest critic, and particularly virulent in denying her the possibility of her having, in the past or present, a life as anything but a servant of the family. Dadi, in her love for her son, pours scorn on the previous existence, the virtue and truthfulness, and every single possible good quality, of her son's wife. Yet, after the bitterest of these attacks—and they are violent, abusive attacks—Rajjo turns the other cheek. She comes with a bottle of oil to massage her mother-in-law's body, or to oil her hair. Sunaina's incredulity is answered with an explanation that leaves us equally incredulous. Dadi and she, says Rajjo, the mother and the daughter-in-law, are one *jati*, one caste or genus. They have to stick together.

One jati? All women? All mothers? All wives? All daughters-in-law? Rajjo's elaboration is on the last two points. When dadi was young, she was physically hurt by dada, repeatedly enough for her to have a bald patch on her head from where he dragged her by the hair. Her own mother-in-law admired her—in dadi's version—but also clearly only because dadi left no stone unturned in her dedication and service of this highly important personage, whose status she is interested in promoting since it is now her own status. So dadi is what she is because it is her fate as a woman, and in turn it is Rajjo's.

Sunaina lacks a vocabulary for saying this. With that, maybe thanks to that, she lacks the confidence for saying it. She remains confused and wondering to the end—where is mai to be found? Who or what was mai? What is her own relationship to mai? Why can she not kick away the past and be free? Why is she held prisoner by the house and mai's memory?

What is mai trying to tell her?

Surely it could not be that Sunaina should be like her. Had Rajjo wanted that, she would have behaved differently towards her daughter and other family members right from the beginning. She stood up to her sister-in-law and father-in-law, antagonised her husband, contradicted (tactfully) her mother-in-law, kept endless secrets, lied and dissimulated, all so that Sunaina could be free to explore and maybe discover 'herself'. We may not be clear about what the mother saw Sunaina as possibly doing. But we can be clear that she did not try to reproduce herself in her daughter.

It is, you might say, simply the mother's love again. That particular impossible quality of maternity: 'I love you but I am so self-sacrificing that I do not want even you for myself. Be free.'

Yes, but this is not as simple as it seems on the surface. This seemingly impossible quality, in fact, says, 'Be free, but you will always be attached. Because you will realise, the stronger you grow in your freedom, that I did not have to hold you by force. You were held by your own will.'

The freedom of Sunaina and Subodh is a reflection of Rajjo's own freedom. She makes herself free by not taking possession on them. We see this in the powerful contrast between her and the others in the family, especially babu. He is utterly weak, even wretched, because he cannot let them go. He cannot be free, of his own possessiveness, his ambitions, and his jealousies.

Rajjo adopts the very difficult course of actually hindering her children in their plan to 'save' her. She saves herself instead, from the inside, as it were, in her own way, with her own priorities in sight. Their guilt at a possible domination is thereby averted as well— something that they are sure to recognise in the afterlife of the novel.

The question of sacrifice illustrates another twist: how mai does not try to reproduce herself in her children, but it does happen. She succeeds somehow in teaching her children her values, including that of self-sacrifice. More importantly, she succeeds in teaching them that hers is not the losing side and the opponent's the winning side. After their years of pursuit of reason, logic, individualism, secularism, modernity, and self-fulfilment, she leaves them—especially her daughter—with serious doubts about 'taking', about self-centredness, about the possible misunderstanding of relationships in the world and balance in the universe. She leaves her daughter wondering about penance, fasting, sacrifice, and bending.

With this we come to what else lies at the heart of *Mai* besides the matter of the mother. It is the saving (*bachana*) of her, the pulling her out (*nikalna*) of the house, the whole business of reform (for which there is no colloquial Hindi word). That is, the novel has two foci: the mother, mai; and the saving of her, or creating of the not-mai. Its two foci are mai and not-mai. Mai is—in the early narrator's voice—hollow, an absence, nothing. Not-mai, or the saving of her, stands for fullness, for choice and personhood.

This could be an abbreviation for the whole narrative of reform in 19th-century India, except that the main actor in the case of *Mai* is, unlike in history, a daughter and not a son. But the novel strives to make the point that the two were a unit initially and made plans to rescue mai as one. If we can overlook this gender differentiation and imagine the siblings as one, what emerges is the simple proposition, 'The children want to improve the mother's lot, but they cannot.' They themselves become free, largely thanks to the mother. They grow beyond the bonds of class, caste, and religion, and are physically free. Then something happens. The daughter decides that she does not want a tug-of-war between them and their mother, and she would like to be neither the winner nor the loser in such a war. So she dedicates her life, instead, to discovering *why* it was that 'improving their mother's lot' was a fallacious proposition.

I am anticipating the next section here when I say that this is a good summary of much of what comprised the reform movements in 19th-century India, and less dramatically, what goes on today. There seem to be two clear-cut sides—the progressive reformers and the conservatives. Between these, women seem to be the passive objects of reform that yield or not to different degrees. Usually they resist, they act as obstacles to reform, they seem incomprehensible in their recalcitrance. In *Mai* both Subodh and Sunaina realise that their pity for their mother has gradually a new element of annoyance in it, but it is Subodh particularly who begins to be bitter about her 'weakness'. Both, however, for most of the book, feel frustrated.

> She simply refused to understand. She refused to change,
> to escape. We would fight for her again and again, and she
> would herself betray us. Babu, from whom we scurried
> around trying to save her, was exactly the one she would
> submit to... She was trapped. She was in chains (pp. 99–100).

And what does Rajjo herself have to say about this? She tells them at different times that this is her work, that the work is in the interest of everyone, not of only the one oppressor or two that they seem to identify, that she enjoys it and takes pleasure in doing it well. The work, precisely speaking, is housework: cooking, serving, childbearing, childrearing, hospitality to guests, and all other odd jobs that arise in the house, such as massaging her mother-in-law's legs or oiling her hair.

As liberal, egalitarian readers, do we not all share her children's dismay that the mother should be slave to this routine of work? That her life should be reformed?

Rajjo does have a reply regarding the satisfactions of her work, but she does not address the other question implied by her children: that she had no choice in being allotted these tasks, that she is additionally abused instead of praised in the performance of them, and that her voice does not figure at all in the chorus of demands and expectations that resound in the house. She seems to understand the abuse as a ritual or cyclical one—one generation to another—and as largely formal. She seems to content herself by being a dignified victim.

In fact, what she is, is an unusual agent of change. She *stops* the cycle of abuse, not merely by not being the kind of mother-in-law that those in the previous generations have been, but by showing no interest in being a mother-in-law at all. She may have liked the idea of her children married and bearing grandchildren, but she does not let it influence her behaviour towards them. She could continue, cyclically, the path shown by bua: since all women are barred in their youth from active choices—in bua's case, of a career, in Rajjo's, presumably, of a marriage of her choice—they use themselves as role models for their juniors. This is the fate of women, they will say. Mai does not give herself these satisfactions. She has other satisfactions. Most of all, perhaps, that she has herself never controlled. Sunaina, at the end of the book, inherits no bitterness or acrimony from her. She will build her own life in unspecified ways.

Similarly, Rajjo is an agent because no matter how preferable silence is to response in the case of some kinds of abuse, she is discriminating. She does not let bullying go beyond a point. One may draw a kind of map of what matters enough to her to speak up for, and what does not. When the abuse is addressed to her children particularly, she retorts and fights back, and is immediately effective. When it is addressed to her other identity, that of a wife, she again acts, and has to be pacified.

But regarding her lack of choice during her whole adult life, starting from her marriage itself, she is silent. So silent that her children do not know anything of her past, even about her parents. How can this be? Why did she not tell her daughter at least? We may suspect that it was because the children were not good listeners. They formed their opinions too strongly, too soon, and she did not want to disturb the trajectory of their lives. They did not give her enough space, enough time. Maybe it was equally because she did not believe the past to be worth anything. Most women in South Asia who are less than 'modern', would date their lives only from their marriage, and consider the time before as an unimportant part of the narrative of their lives. If so, then Rajjo, in considering her past 'nothing', is indeed, as her children imagine, 'nothing'. Their desire to rescue her includes giving her a past, and if their failure in this is partly due to their insensitivity, it is also partly due to Rajjo's refusal to pursue their vision.

But Rajjo, with the limited past that she has—exactly one letter, and then the reawakened desire of her father to see his granddaughter—is not a non-actor. She keeps the letter instead of destroying it, and somehow by the end, conveys to her children that they should listen more carefully to the whispers of the past.

Now, if we have to interpret this particular stand of women like Rajjo—I will not speak or fight for what you think I should be—and interpret it in a way different to the rational, reformist, children, that is, different to the early Sunaina and closer to the later Sunaina, we may come up with something like this. Women have their calculations of what the spaces for them are, where their freedoms lie, and how certain satisfactions may be maximised through certain manipulations. They, too, wish for change on many counts. But, while we know the scattered efforts of women in the history of reform that were more or less direct in nature, we lack a vocabulary for stating, and a methodology for uncovering, the 'efforts' that were less than 'direct'. In *Mai*, as we see, it would be a fallacy to say that the mother, Rajjo, does *nothing* towards her own emancipation and only hinders her children's efforts—as certainly seems to be the blunt case on the surface. It seems to me that Rajjo transmits the burdens of her containment, her repression, her burdens, very effectively. She *makes* herself a bent, pitiful creature. She *uses*, to put it in its most daring form, her children as weapons in her fight against society. But she does not reveal this, maybe does not admit it to herself, and they, certainly, imagine that they are the ones in charge, the ones with a vision. What they do not grasp, and what all of us scholars of the reforms in 19th-century India have not grasped, is that a woman and her life is not *raw data*, to be then taken up and interpreted by the reformer. She and her life are already *interpreted*, and in analogy with the informant's interaction with the ethnographer, the resulting text—in our case, reform or change—is the product of this interaction. The story of the reforms of 19th-century India is largely a story of the wills of those to be reformed, who, like

Rajjo, partly taught others what had to be reformed, and largely refused to be taught themselves.

In addition, there is another kind of reform that might go unnoticed, that of ending certain cycles and not passing on cruel or thoughtless treatment received by oneself to others structurally similarly placed. Just as abuse towards women comes from women as much as men, one could wake up and see that perhaps reform of women's conditions comes from women as much as men.

There are these different aspects to the mother, then. She seemingly 'sacrifices' for her children to be 'free'; it would be more accurate to say that she *labours*. She could do this with physical labour, which might bend or break her body. She could do it with nurture and support. More subtly, she does it often not by fighting but by resisting getting involved in fighting.

She reveals to the children what is so abused about her life, what is empty, chained, in pain. Again, she does this not through direct statement, through no strategy that anybody can point to or cite. But she shows what she wants to, although they do not always realise or read it as such.

At the same time, she does not make those whom she is educating and bringing up, sufferers of the same fate that she has had. Indeed, she reverses their future for them.

Finally, she has her own life and existence that is quite separate from them, even unknown to them, even unguessed by them. She can even scold them about belittling her hidden life, but typically she is closed about it. To their regret, they realise only later that not only did she have a life of her own, but that she had many sources of strength.

~

We must try to resolve this confusion about silence as well. Is silence weakness, or is it strength? Is it voluntary or involuntary? Is it something that emanates from the subject, or is it a product of the subject's associates' and reformers' inability to comprehend messages?

Rajjo's silence is interpreted by different characters differently. Babu sees it as the result of her lack of education (about which he is imprecise) and her insufficient exposure to the world. This, together with her subservient personality, results for him in her seeming a supremely dumb, passive object, comparable to a round eggplant rolling around on a plate, or a spoutless pot that can be pushed in any direction one wishes. Subodh labels his mother's silence 'weakness', calls her a 'weakling', and shouts at her to speak, to speak out, to say something. Sunaina hesitates to label her mother's silence as anything. She notices instead the calm that accompanies the silence, the dignity on the face, the strength of the silence contrasted to the incessant nagging from others.

Rajjo has her own explanation for her silence. She might say, shortly, 'I have nothing to say,' when Subodh, particularly, shouts at her, but she elaborates, tellingly, 'If I listen to one side, I have to listen to others as well. Then it is difficult to act.' This importance of hesitating, of balance, is exactly what Sunaina discovers as she instinctively shies away from being either a 'victor' or a 'loser'.

The silence is contrasted mildly with dada's garrulousness, loud voice, love of monologue, authoritarianism and opinionated personality. Where he would belittle others, including for their caste or family, Rajjo silently respects them. Where he bullies, she wins over. Where he fails to communicate, she succeeds.

The silence is more clearly contrasted with dadi's common speech, her selfish formulations, and her screams and efforts to draw attention to herself in pain. Rajjo is in pain too, but silently. She works much harder than dadi, but unnoticed. She seems to accept victimisation as the target of dadi's sarcasm, but the sarcasm is such that silence could be the only dignified response.

Most of all, the silence is clearly contrasted with babu's whimpering and whining, his confused statements and contradictory propositions. He tries various ruses to eavesdrop and elicit information, whereas mai in her silence has to try none—she gets the information she wants. He is evasive in spite of his volubility, and she is direct in spite of her silence.

Finally, the silence is contrasted with Rajjo's own clear speech at points when strictly necessary—but also, one must not forget, with her own ordinary joking and laughter with her children, proof that they were a threesome for them, and for us that she was simply an ordinary person and no tight-lipped heroine.

Silence certainly emerges as a communicative practice, one of many, and one used strategically and meaningfully. Given the way that the novel makes its comparisons and contrasts, and given all the implicit and explicit contextualisations of silence, we are obliged to realise that silence is in no way inferior to other practices, but is stronger, more voluntary, and deserving of much soul-searching on the part of others.

~

Finally, we have to take seriously another problem that the matter of the mother gives rise to: of interpretation versus life. I state it as baldly as this because domination works in both and is not adequately recognised as such. I have suggested above that our 'natural' interpretation of a mother like Rajjo, as of her children, is that she is weak, but that other interpretations should be formulated whereby her own spaces and strengths are recognised. Now I wish to suggest that while in interpretation we must thus 'bow down' to mai, to the 'silent, repressed woman', and change the whole interpretation of reform, passivity, and freedom in 19th-century India, we must equally question what we want women to *be*. *Should* women be like Rajjo? Strong, dignified, and good. But also: forced to marry against their will, in parda all their lives, abused by their parents-in-law, ignored and poorly treated by their husbands? I have deliberately kept these definitions to the barest, and excluded mention of 'power', 'strength', 'freedom', and so on. I think I may presume to suggest that all the readers of this text would agree that women should *not* be in this position. Therefore, what the dilemma seems to resolve itself to is the following question: would the cause of women be better served by critiquing their existing conditions, or would it be better served by showing a sensitivity to its hidden compensations and actual positive features?

It would seem that to critique means to ignore some things, to distort others, and to finally draw back from balanced assessment. It would seem that to speak with respect and sensitivity means to hold double standards: some things are all right for others and we even appreciate them, but we would not like them for ourselves. Where we interpret a life positively, we refrain from living that life.

This seemingly familiar feminist dilemma itself gets a new twist by looking at the case of mai, and also gets a new energy in a possible impact on the studies of reform and social change in India. The new twist for feminism would be to see how, even within certain repressive structures, women can not only tolerate and act for themselves, but actively change the course of the future by refusing to participate in the repression. Many widows, as I have found, wished precisely to change the future for other potential widows like themselves (Kumar 1992). Then, the history of 'reform movements', as they are called, and indeed the whole history of modern India, would benefit from an enlargement of its methodology, inspired by a feminist search for not only women's action and agency that is identifiable as such, but that which is more daringly defined as such.

Why, one may ask, should one bother? Novels are read not for us to judge whether we would choose the protagonist's life for ourselves. Obviously the discourse is being shifted here to one of the subject position in history. Doing that, are we not justified in inquiring after the positioning of the self, the actor, vis-a-vis that which is being studied, interpreted, reformed? In *Mai*, the positioning is as follows: young man and young woman want to reform their mother. They understand the mother as pitiable. At a certain point, the young man and young woman part company with each other: he continues to regard the mother as before, she revises her perspective to wonder whether the problem was as simple as had seemed. The book ends with her dilemma.

Although the gendering of the two reformers perhaps overstates the case—the siblings could have been two sisters and behaved exactly as do this brother and sister—one crucial factor here is certainly gender. Sunaina has the body and, she fears, the spirit of her mother, and previous ancestresses. Subodh has neither. He has inherited, if anything, his grandfather's roaring voice and spirit. Sunaina therefore has an advantage. But we can do away with this asset and perfectly well suggest that an observer of *either* sex could come around to seeing the problem as not that simple, the strong saving the weak. It is also the problem of vision and strength, and of understanding.

To sum up, then: *Mai* suggests a methodology for pursuing the mother, for asking a question and problematising whose question it is. Given that it does not give the mother a direct voice, it might seem to confine her as the object of our gaze. But some of us will feel, I think, that it is not we watching and objectifying mai, but it is rather she, throughout the book, watching others, albeit non-judgementally.

The problem is actually equally ours. For the book and its project it may be that of the 'daughterly perspective'. Its solution? Not to re-instate the mother as the subject, but the future telling of the story by the mother and daughter together, the reformer and the reformed. For us the problem is how to accept being non-judgemental, passive as that position seems. The solution? To extend the topic of study into the methodology for studying it.

M*ai* does what every good novel does: it serves as brilliant ethnography. It creates a world that convinces us of its reality. It is full of people with energy and conflict, it has tastes and sounds, it has clashes and resolutions, and weaves a complex net of relations between people, emotions, artefacts, and symbols. There is the credibility of the complexity, untidiness, and motion, but also the structure, weight, and holism of everyday life. In this sense, it does, like every good piece of fiction, more than what ethnography does, because the latter, counter-intuitively, aims to tidy up, simplify, render inert and stable, and classify elegantly, and in the process, render what we know as 'life' less credibly. Since I am appreciative of the particular tasks of ethnographers, I will not belabour this point. What concerns me here is not any comparison, implicit or explicit, but how social scientists (anthropologists, sociologists, political scientists, historians, and others) might 'use' *Mai*. Again, I am not concerned with whether they should or should not, and whether it is good or proper to do so. I recognise that fiction is used all the time by social scientists, in the classroom and in writings, and want to explore one particular case of how it could be so used.

It is easy to see that the novel works on two levels: the literal and the metaphorical. It is literally about a family in a north Indian small town over three generations, their house, fields and orchards, their place in society, the children's education and escape to wider horizons, and the inner hierarchies of the family where their mother is particularly the victim. It tells us about caste, religion, gender, colonialism, and modernity—all the staples of various branches of South Asian studies.

What it does additionally is to present layer upon layer of data that we can read metaphorically as well as literally.

The house is a metaphor for domination, repression, and freedom, at different times. The food is a metaphor for choice, service, and modernity in various contexts. Clothes are multivocal. The body can symbolise diverse states of being. Language, speech, and silence tell us more than they seem to on the surface.

The house has the structure of a courtyard, lined by verandahs and rooms facing inside, a passage from the inside to the outside, and an external *baithak* or sitting room where hospitality reigns. This is the design we known from histories and ethnographies, for some of us from travel and living in India. What does it do to human relations? It comments on them, of course. But, as *Mai* allows us to glimpse, it constructs them also. There is an active interaction of the house design with human lives, even a causal relationship. Dadi, when broken-hipped and in pain, can still lie there on a chaise lounge and supervise domestic activities with her sharp tongue the whole day. If she had a separate room she would be isolated and at the mercy of those who chose to come and sit by her.

Dada, like dadi, enjoys the pleasures of age and retirement: talk, food, bossing, pontification, and music. He entertains who he likes and gets what he wants. That he does not have a closed room to bathe in and was thus observed by his grandchildren is a minor disadvantage. He is the one who has honed the inside-outside pattern to perfection. The inside is both literal—no women folk ever appear outside—and metaphorical: women do not sing or dance or do anything 'public'. Nothing in their inside should turn to the outside except, ironically, their teeth.

It is equally true, though unstated, that dada, the archetypical male, would not appear inside. Babu does, but in passing, to eat, to change, to greet his mother every day and chat with her, to pass to his wife purchases for the house. He has his own room there, though at some times he sleeps in dada's. Dada does not have a room inside. It is fair to say that in terms of 'freedom', the women are free in their own specialised space as the men are in theirs. Yes, the 'outside' does sound bigger. It allures as open and unfettered. The idea of escaping from inside to outside grows with the children. But, as Sunaina discovers, it does not benefit the bird in the sky to have a vast expanse around her, if she can cover only a small compass anyway, and sometimes, as she observes, not even that, but flutter her wings in the air and remain stationary.

Mai, of course, does not need a house for confinement; she is in a parda of her own. And yet it is the very design of the kitchen, the storeroom, and the courtyard that necessitates her being bent over always. She develops a weak spine—both metaphorically and literally—from always having to pick up, clean, sort out, grind, mix, cut, and cook things bent over. And in her case the open location of these activities is not an obvious advantage. She can always be observed by dadi, who keeps up a running commentary on what she observes, ironical and implicitly critical. If mai had a closed kitchen with modern counters, she would not only have never bent over, she would have had the privacy to order her activities in her own way.

There are mixed blessings for her in other aspects of the design. There is no master bedroom in the house, which would have of course created a twosome on the one hand and a separation from the children on the other. Like this, she stands alone, supported progressively by her children, but certainly not as a conjugal couple with her husband unless at the rare times of going out to the club. On the other hand she does not have to spend a lot of time with him, including at night, and can indulge in horseplay and crazy jokes with her son and daughter as a threesome. In 'their' room, theirs and hers. The absence of a conjugal bedroom may suggest pre-modernity and the attendant lack of freedom and privacy to some. But the novel makes it clear that freedom may lie in sharing with the children instead of the spouse. Certainly companionate marriage has not been discovered by the adults in the novel, though there is a discernible progress through the generations: bua and phupha, and babu and mai have discovered it more than dada and dadi, and Sunaina and Subodh will no doubt go on to discover it far more than any of these.

The children have infinite resources for freedom. They have the fields, the roof, the courtyard, everywhere except beyond the gates, where they go only with permission or under escort. Their experience of animals, of fruits and vegetables, no less than of human activities, is a product of the house design. When they grow up and leave, it is the house the haunts them, particularly the roof, its views, low hanging branches, the fields, the trees around, the changing seasons. In each memory, located physically in the house, is the spirit of mai.

The house has in a way created mai, at the least by giving her a bad spine. But it is mai who has created the house, and neither can be said to be a prior creation. The way the house runs and every detail of its functioning is mai's personal responsibility. It runs one way when dada and dadi are alive, and another after their death— in both cases because mai wills it so. It is not mindless labour, it is not habit, and it is not simple-minded service on her part. It is what she is: someone who thinks of the house and its functioning as hers. Her activity in this regard is re-confirmed by her absence outside the house.

The house can also then be viewed as a power engine for generating sensibilities, practices, and selves, but, importantly, a power engine masterminded by mai. If we are going to make the identification of mother with home, domesticity, and the inside, as it seems from all evidence that we have to do, then we should at least re-evaluate the home with some sensitivity. Sunaina supplies us with some clues by observing at regular intervals throughout the book that she simply had not thought about the apparent contradiction of mai's obvious strength in the middle of her more apparent weakness. Or, as she puts it yet more relevantly, she had not thought about the thought.

But the house goes beyond mai. There is an identification of the house with childhood, and with life itself. Like one's childhood and one's life, the house is suffused with something extra-material, something mystery-filled, maybe ghost-like. Old, dead ancestors appear in it, fogs and clouds enter its doors and windows, its walls echo with voices, its corners look on as if with eyes. To use a familiar image for Hindi filmgoers,

> ma ka dil ban ke kabhi sine se lag jata hai tu
> phir kabhi nanhi si bitiya ban ke yaad ata hai tu

> (You take me sometimes to your bosom like a mother;
> then at other times you haunt me as if you were my
> little daughter)

—it is both mother/parent and daughter/child in turn. It bears the children, it binds them, it makes them grow, it suffocates them. All they dream of is escaping it. When they escape, all they dream of is returning to it. When they are almost free, chance brings them back and binds them to it. It may not be obvious why they feel so rooted in it. The house, even while a reflection of mai and the life she has created for the children, has an independent existence: its life revolves like the seasons and continues beyond mai. But of course it is not beyond history, and when the time comes, it becomes a ruin and is abandoned by all.

We certainly have insufficient discussion in Anthropology yet of how spaces work, how homes are created, lost, and remembered, how homes can control lives, and how they can become, even more than the parent, the locus of childhood and the past. *Mai* reminds us of this lack.

In the history of modern India, the 'public' and the 'private' are supposed to be colonial, modern creations. The novel does not shed direct light on the subject, but certainly gives us interesting insights into their working. When change has to be shown, it is through the 'creation' of a modern bathroom: what has never been private before is made so by modernity. The creation of 'privacy' through doors and partitions , as in the new dining room and bathrooms, may be the signifier of modernity, but has multi-layered repercussions. Mai is the ultimate private person. Her observance of privacy is such that even her daughter has never seen so much as her naked back. Is this modern or pre-modern? We have noted that husbands and wives do not have private bedrooms, but the children and mai do. Should we interpret conjugal privacy as modern and parent-child privacy as pre-modern?

A significant denoter of modernity is the written word. The two ways in which this appears in the novel are as forms: application forms to be signed and acceptance forms to be received, and as letters. Forms are markers of passage from one phase of life to another, signed by the more cooperative parent, mai, who thus makes possible all the important changes in the lives of her children. Acceptance forms are received by her 'sacrifice' and that of those emulating her. Letters are the ultimate bearers of truth. Mai begins to write one but never does write it, and her children suspect it was a farewell note to a suicide or an escape. She has received exactly one letter ever, and for this she has no private repository. The fire-hot messenger from her past is merely tucked away within the yellowing paper of a photo frame. Sunaina writes many, by contrast, about her new life and all its dramatic events, and receives many, including from boyfriends. These are her private property, and must not be opened or read by anyone. One could suggest that modern education has made the difference.

The pre-modern Indian, the 'essential' Indian of E.M. Forster who cannot resist idly perusing a letter lying on mantelpiece while awaiting his host, and the babu who deliberately reads every letter received by his children, is replaced by the modern Indian who expects and demands that what is addressed to her should be for her eyes only. But this suggestion is belied by the character of mai. She is not modern-educated, but she fully and sincerely respects the privacy of letters. Similarly she respects other 'modern' conventions, of the privacy and inviolability of friendships and other love relationships.

What dominates the novel, the reader may feel, is the constant creation of food. From the very beginning people are what they eat, except mai, who is what she cooks. Dada and dadi's gourmet tastes mark them out as hedonists, as old world non-realistic self-indulgers, who scoff at mundane notions of diet and exercise.

The contrast between East and West, old and new, is drawn simply and lightly. Most importantly, it is not the only line of division. That is, foods could be classified according to: whether they were approved by dadi or not; easy for mai or not; nutritious according to Sunaina or not; digestible by babu or not. A food from 'England' or 'the village' would be better represented on these grids rather than as 'Indian' or 'Western', modern or pre-modern. Dadi demonstrates perfectly how one could enjoy any 'Western' or modern dish without making a dent in her 'indigenous' preferences. Sunaina and Subodh, when both emancipated and free, miss their old foods and, it is implied, do not give them up.

Dada and dadi's abandon with food reflects not only their carelessness with their own health, but their carelessness with others' convenience as well. Subodh and Sunaina are obliged to eat over-greasy, over-cooked foods, and mai, most of all, to produce whatever may strike the fancy of the elders, so that she is 'always cooking'. Babu, in his spartan choices, displays the complicated nature of domination. It is not always with fierceness and loudness that domination is exercised, but with gentleness and quietness as well. His food demands are the opposite of dada and dadi's, but equally exploitative of mai.

As for other treasures in the novel about other staples of enquiry: caste, language, religion, the rural–urban contrast, colonialism, and reform, I do not think I would like to labour them, but simply to suggest their potential.

Caste is a shadow presence throughout the book—as one may argue it is in India itself—through allusions to servants, uncleanliness, the outside, people's pasts and futures, and the unembarrassed prejudices of dada's jokes. Mai does not have to be a modern, educated character, simply a humane, practical one, for her to have the dirty dishes scrubbed by a sweeper woman when necessary. Equally, we can imagine that dada, for all his prejudices, would not forfeit the pleasures of music or conversation—or rather, his monologues to a captive audience—simply because the people in his sitting room belonged to castes self-declaredly lower to his own.

The languages in the house include chiefly Bhojpuri, 'clean' Hindi, and English, and then some mixtures of these. The range from them is plotted on an axis of education and exposure to the outside. Dadi is presumably unlettered and speaks only a rural dialect, which this translator has, unfortunately, no talent to represent in another code. Her being uneducated means no lowering of her power or status, no shortcoming in her self-confidence, and no lack of knowledge on any topic of relevance, from housekeeping to religion to ethics.

Mai is a First Arts pass, that is, class 12, and speaks clean Hindi like her husband and father-in-law, who have seen the world. She dresses the same as her mother-in-law, in a traditional style *sidha palla* (the sari end over her right shoulder), and acts the same as home-maker and server, but *speaks* differently to her. We can see this difference in language and speech reflected in the unmitigated suspicion that dadi harbours towards mai. She is even accused of corresponding with her former suitor, one suspects because of her education.

Babu and dada, in spite of their firm adherence to the superiority of age and sex, are consumed with a love of the symbols of modernity, most of all the English language. To some extent dadi and mai share this love as well, but they have almost nothing to lose. The story of dada and babu's losses at the feet of the goddess of English, as it were, is in a way the narrative of whole of modern India. Did not every generation in turn feel that the next generation should learn English and its wider culture better than themselves, and that this learning would somehow be confined to a technical mastery and not spill over to the rest of life? That the young man or woman would merely attend a fancy college but not then take dreams of freedom seriously and want to break away from 'home'? That the young person would not discover a 'self' that had to be further discovered and satisfied, rather than be satisfied with the self reproduced on the model of his or her forbears?

As I see it, every generation of the educated classes in India has done this to different extents (Kumar 2000) and has refused to face the obvious conclusions to be drawn from the lessons of other generations. That no one can learn merely a language. When the language learnt stands for a culture, then is it particularly difficult not to take what 'words stand for' to heart. It is not just that Sunaina and Subodh become fluent in English and use English words. It is that they take 'English' or 'Western' concepts of the self utterly seriously, seek freedoms and discover truths that come with their new language. There is thus, in the book, not merely the play of Bhojpuri, Hindi, and English languages and their mixtures, but the play of Bhojpuri, Hindi, and English discourses and their mixtures.

The rural–urban continuum is related to that of the languages, in that the rural end is connected to Bhojpuri, and the urban, culminating in London, to English. The rural–urban contrast is drawn fleetingly with regard to the nature of consumption in the small town, displaying its rural poverty of taste in some of its markets and cinema halls. But it is drawn more powerfully with regard to the town's village-like lack of sophisticated educational institutions. Sunnyside Convent does have nuns, but they read Barbara Cartland. Only Subodh's school in the larger city can teach English properly and has all the classics in its library. Students broaden their minds on them and develop an intimacy with England along the way, and so do the women in their family through their assistance.

Then there is the insight that a novel like *Mai* gives us into the meanings of religion in India today. Rajjo, as the dutiful daughter-in-law of a high caste Hindu family, keeps scores of fasts, almost exclusively for her husband's and son's well-being, and like all such wives and mothers, *believes* in keeping them. The power that accrues from fasts and the accompanying lifestyle, as I argue elsewhere (Kumar 1992) includes both the power of the image of such a person (even dadi respects her daughter-in-law for her lifestyle) and the internal power of the ascetic whose energies are increased by such concentration. Sunaina believes that the image is fallacious, but that the internal power is real. A summation, we might say, of a change in Hinduism, which is powerful as a social structure but not as a cognitive structure.

Babu fasts and prays too, but with an evocatively described reliance on his wife's prior preparations, and a simple pleasure in the culmination of the fast. The description of his eating can make us only relate to him with bemusement. There is, by contrast, no description-ever-of what mai enjoys, only of what she wants to eat because it is stale or leftover. But babu has another hang-up: superstition. He takes literally prohibitions against proceeding with an action in the face of a sneeze or other obstacle, and more seriously, is devoted to a holy man. None of the holy man's miracles will hold up to enquiry, but babu is not only simple-minded enough to never challenge them, he goes one step further and claims that his particular guru is the origin of all religions everywhere. His exaggerated, simple-minded religiosity is a counterpoint to the suave pleasures of dada, to the aesthetically enjoyable practices of mai, to the mechanical scriptural recitations of dadi, and to the rationalistic questioning of the brother and sister. If we add to this the professionalism of the guru, and the imputed backwardness of the servants Hardeyi and Bhondu, we might have exhausted the larger part of the varieties of religious practice in India.

An important dimension of Rajjo's character is her refusal to take up the gauntlet thrown by her husband regarding the dangers of the various liaisons of their children. The one with the foreigner is dangerous, but the really threatening one is the one with the Muslim. Who is he, how serious is Sunaina, is she planning to marry him? These are babu's questions but no amount of prodding from him will make mai ask them of Sunaina. This is the other dimension of 'religion' and 'rationality' in 'India'. A relatively uneducated, untravelled person like Rajjo, herself cast as a shadow and a victim, does not have any problem in respecting her daughter and daughter's choices of friends, no matter who or what they are. She does not ever pass judgement but waits patiently for them to reveal themselves, and then accepts and reciprocates what she likes and simply ignores the rest. Respect for 'difference', it is suggested, does not lie only with the modern, nor, paradoxically, does humanism, but rather the reverse.

Mai comments on the colonial aspect of India equally succinctly. The patriarch, dada, has made his image as a 'freedom fighter', and informally as well, bested several Englishmen at various things, even while doing whatever is necessary in the British mode, such as having a portrait made, or having dadi get an artificial hip. He is resolutely non-anglicised in his lifestyle, to the extent of having a distaste for gadgets, and a pronounced taste for 'feudal' servitude and hierarchy. It is a familiar personage, one that makes us question the virtues of resistance to modernity, even if it is colonial modernity.

Babu's is the other resistance, but similarly convoluted. He prefers his wife in parda, his daughter silent, and he himself subservient to his father. He worships a godman, eats austerely, and is the proverbial good son. But he frequents the club, and admires his son's burgeoning competence in a global world.

Close in importance to the major themes of house and food is the body. Many bodies 'break' at different points and it is difficult to classify them simply. Indeed they work towards different purposes. The longest lasting is the problem of Rajjo's body. Rajjo stoops, and her stooping, from the first line of the book, is a metaphor for a weak will. That she is always bent over is her choice and leads, as expected, to constant, incurable pain and a habit she cannot and will not change. It goes with her sacrificing herself and her putting herself second before all, to prostrate herself metaphorically before all, to negate herself in favour of their needs and wishes. To a historian of British India, the metaphor evokes the similarity between women and the colony. The colonised were seen, and to some extent grew to see themselves, as 'small', 'servile', 'effeminate', as opposed to the colonisers, who were tall, upright, and manly.

Dadi's hip breaks in a fall and her limp and accompanying enforced leisure is merely a part of her aging. But, important to note, the aging is not a mental aging at all. Even without teeth and in spite of the doctor's orders, she eats with gusto and adores everything new. Similarly she can keep up her matriarchal discipline in the house without the use of good legs. We understand that her disability is an asset to her in disguise, because she now cannot do any work and mai, perforce, must do everything.

Babu's case tells us a great deal about the sources of women's strength, therefore, of their weakness. He becomes disabled in an accident and mai spends the rest of his life waiting on a helpless invalid. The significance of this lies in the rude extension of her servitude by fate. She cannot do anything but be at babu's side all the time now, even to the point of having to now share the same bedroom—which was one bond she had been free from so far. Yet, mai is not unhappy. To be at the helm of affairs brings out her hitherto dominated strengths. She speaks louder, she commands, she expects and gets obedience. The death or invalid status of the husband can become, we realise, a new lease of life for the wife or widow. The once-powerful man can become an empowering figure for the woman when broken. There is a new freedom and vitality for the female with the death, or disfigurement, of the male—as Edna St. Vincent Millay's poem describes, at the collapse of the buck, about 'Life, looking out attentive from the eyes of the doe' (Millay 1928: 228).

So, Rajjo was not *inherently* a spineless creature as the author seemed to have suggested. Indeed, as I write, I look out of the window (in India) and see in the space of one minute two working women striding along with baskets on their heads. They walk tall and could be models in a finishing school. A question regarding being 'bent over' comes to mind. Does the posture of the women get transferred to their actual strength, in their family, community, and world-at-large? If they are strong and straight in their walk, surely they do not cook and serve others at home *bent over*? If they don't, if they remain as deliberately upright as on the road, then we know we are dealing with a class issue. Rajjo is what she is because she is part of a certain kind of middle class, patriarchal household. Hers is not the problem of 'Indian women', or of 'mothers', and certainly not of 'women'.

But if they do, that is if the working women I observe are straight-backed on the street and bent over at home, then we must question the co-relation between physical cowering and psychological cowering. Bending over may be a habit for the woman, may be even a convenient habit; it may be a pose or attitude; it may transmit some gratification as of a role well played, a value well enforced, a self satisfaction enjoyed. It does not denote that she is cowering inside, or is actually subordinating herself. It could be like the parda, or any other playacting, device, or impersonation. It has its uses and conveniences. You observe yourself dong it. It does not make you into something that you are not. Yes, it could become oppressive if, like a permanent mask, there is no escape from it. But it could have its compensations.

Rajjo's bending over seems to be of this latter kind. She is in fact the strongest character in the book, insofar as she has amazing principles that she never betrays regarding her children's privacy, their right to decide and choose, and the dignity inherent in them and indeed in every human being. She is even heroic and is certainly enviable in this strength of hers. Plus she is superlative at the more predictable things: keeping everything synchronised and harmonious in the house, everyone satisfied, all wheels oiled and rolling.

Again, we are not surprised. We come back to the matter of the mother. Mothers are known to have strengths, most ostensibly to decide, control, manipulate—none of which is particularly hidden. Yet they seem to be puppets who dance to everyone's tune, even when they are known to have solid cores, definite shapes, and rock-hard resistances. We have repeatedly suspected that mothers are pretending to more weakness than they deserve pity for.

The feminist reader is given a puzzle, which is exactly what the social scientist must deal with. Mai, the mother, is not as weak or helpless or in need of rescuing as would seem by every objective criteria. She has immense reservoirs of strength, which can be observed at odd times and even all the time with some insight. But besides that, there is a problem of definition. What is strength? What is bondage and what freedom? If Rajjo does not need to be rescued, is it because she is placid and ignorant and suffers from false consciousness; or is it because the narrator has few tools of empathy and experience to interpret the rewards of Rajjo's life as being lived by her? Who is wrong, the old/'traditional'/unquestioning woman or the young/'modern'/questioning woman?

The author seems to pronounce judgement in favour of the old, and seems to describe the younger woman as regretting her simplified, one-dimensional view of mai. But, do we not feel convinced that, given the nature of the house, her husband, her in-laws, and her duties, Rajjo is indeed confined? She had a lover once and cannot even write to him or see him again. She is belittled as a cook and housewife by her mother-in-law. She is forbidden to hum or sing, to dress up or to go out, by her husband and father-in-law in turn. She is supposed to have no powers to take decisions and is therefore not expected to. Only when the older people die off and her own husband gets bed-ridden does she take more and more decisions, explores more of her personality. This is a familiar generational cycle for Indian women. But she does not have even a *name*, and she does not care that her daughter, too, has one that will partly be erased. Between her cooking and feeding, no matter how excellently, and her namelessness and her silences, no matter how peaceable, do we not pity her?

Maybe it just underlines the hidden side of history, what many historians would acknowledge but not do anything about. And others besides historians, because

> maternity has always been the repressed term in the family plot. Just as the matronymic is blanked out by the patronymic, just as the mother's lineage is forfeited to the father's, and just as maternal discourse has been governed by paternal law, so the mother herself has had to die to narrative possibility. Associated with blood, flesh, materiality, she has appeared so intransigently imminent

that literary, indeed cultural, authority has been predicated
on a transcendence or a repudiation of her being (Gilbert
and Gubar 1994: 378).

Mai presents us with a mother-heroine, like Sethe (Morrison 1987),
who can leave us questioning the joys of motherhood.

If this can remain an open matter—to pity or not to pity
Rajjo—then we have literature here that teaches social scientists
something. It supports my long-felt agreement with what Virginia
Woolf says in *The Pargiters*: 'It would be far easier to write history
[than fiction, but] that method of telling the truth seems to me so
elementary, and so clumsy, that I prefer, where truth is important,
to write fiction' (Woolf 1997: 9).

This may be easier said of the matter of the mother than all
the other ethnographic stuff in the novel. After all, whose is the
representative voice on 'India'—the author's, the narrator's, the
characters'? How do we readers know it speaks with authority? At
which point should we suspend our disbelief willingly?

I am interested in childhood and mothering and associated
processes. I recollect, on reading *The God of Small Things* that
while I loved the depiction of childhood in that novel, I thought
there had been a grievous mistake in drawing the character of
the mother and her lover. Or, one could have a familiarity or even
intimacy with a place or a people and therefore either trust the
author, or suspect the author of making a mistake regarding them.
I know weavers, and specially the weavers of Banaras, and Abdul
Bismillah in *Jhini Jhini Bini Chadariya* gives a masterful portrayal
that wins my sincerest admiration and envy. But I know Lucknow
too and feel little empathy for Amritlal Nagar's Lucknow. Because
I know too little? Because I do not know the kinds of people he is
writing about? Because he has failed?

What this tells me is to be prepared for what the fiction text
does versus what the social science text does, and what each does

not. The former does not systematise, theorise, or generalise. It is not in search of reality, because it is reality—reality lies within it. The latter worries about all exceptions (if not in the text itself, then in the critique of it). It wants to present what reality is, either as statement or as negation. Because a text, as Umberto Eco would say, is a lazy machine that expects the reader to do some of its work, the reader must assess her own needs and expectations when approaching the text, and of course, competence. Perhaps we may say that there is a complementarity of emotion and objectivity that has to be supplied to the text and by the text, and the particular mixture must be worked out in each case.

Having said all of which, I would not say that I *know* what a work of fiction is, or what a social science text is, or wherein lies the exact difference between them.

PART III

On Translation

I am uncomfortable with the role I seem to be performing—that of the critic, certain of the 'nature' of literature and of the way to read it, convinced of the mimetic view of literature, holding the belief, as it were, that: 'The task of literature is to render life, experience, and emotion in a potent way; the job of criticism is to reveal the true value and meaning of the rendition—a rendition at once contained within the literary work any yet, paradoxically, needing the critical act to reveal it' (Rice and Waugh 1989: 2–3).

This humanist, empiricist, and idealist view that takes language to be transparent and experience to be prior, is exactly what I would like to eschew. Unfortunately, I do not know of a way to do so as a translator, and as a social scientist who wants to deliberately 'use' *Mai*. I accept that my translation is an interpretation and, along with this more direct discussion, is obliged to repeat the endlessly repetitive agenda that reading literature comprises, never to reach a certain or final reading of the text, and certainly not an explanation of it.

Mai is profound interest to me because it does at the level of fiction what I strive to do through history and anthropology: to show that although public voices 'decree that the course of history should shape itself this way or that way, being manfully determined to control the course of events', private domestic lives move silently forward, whose importance we do not always have a vocabulary to convey (Woolf 1978: 172, in Gilbert and Gubar 1994: 17). The strength of supposed weakness, the splendour of supposed dullness, the paradox inherent at the heart of power, is what many vocabularies do convey, but social science can do only approximately. Marianne Moore is only one instance of many artists when she emphasises this paradox, as when celebrating, beyond the envious will to self-aggrandisement that constructs history, 'the power of relinquishing/what one would keep; that is freedom' (Moore 1967: 144).

Then it is of interest to me because *Mai* is a feminist novel, not only a novel about women or speaking to women. Its feminism works at different levels. It takes gender to be socially constructed, and therefore capable of being reconstructed. Rajjo is brought to our consciousness, through the burgeoning consciousness of her daughter, as someone with a past, someone who was many things in potentio before she became 'only' a wife, daughter-in-law, and mother, although she seems to be only these things par excellence. She herself does not cultivate these identities in her daughter.

Mai uses some of the tropes of feminist writing, such as the narrativising and problematising of the past. *Mai* is about the past, seemingly about a world passed and gone, but actually about its construction, what it *seemed*, its meanings, its uses.

The protagonist, while thus establishing her relationship to the past, breaks with it and redefines it in overt ways. The mother is herself not very educated, does not read or paint or discuss, and equates the world outside her kitchen with 'school and college'. The aunt scoffs at painting. The grandmother despises everything that is not measurable by the yardsticks of men, specially her son. The daughter, in contrast, begins to paint to portray facelessness and (to write?) to give voice to silences. She is doing so not to produce a commercially marketable cultural artefact (as her brother wants to push her to do) but to express herself. This expression runs into a lot of trouble with questioning of the relative gain and loss. She gains freedoms, but there is suspicion of a possible 'loss of women's inheritance' (Jacobus 1979: 10).

Lastly, it could be seen to be feminist in a narrower sense. The author and translator/critic of the book are certainly consciously producing cultural artefacts, but through them both coming to terms with the paradoxes of 'woman' and breaking in little possible ways with historically established denials of women to artistic and literary discourse. The writing itself both articulates protest and enacts it. But even so, they make themselves part of the universal process of the 'historical' and the articulated feeding off the 'a-historical' and the muted. It is the condition of the 'ordinary woman's life' that they write about. It is a presentation and interpretation of that which bestows importance on 'the ordinary woman' but also importance, through her non-subjective presence, on the author and translator (Woolf 1967: 142).

The question is a large and all-encompassing one for women and feminism, partly intuited, partly understood. Strength can well lie outside oneself, in connections with details 'outside', typically humbler and duller than 'History'. Whether this is a durable difference appropriately labelled 'the feminine', or only historically so, it is certainly a deliberate and reflexive difference with others sorts of strengths.

∼

As if I was already not being ambitious enough in this commentary, I cannot resist musing aloud on my experience with translating, particularly with the transitions of a cultural nature that occur when translating from Hindi to English.

The reason I am interested in the Hindi to English question is because of its embeddedness in a politics. The politics arises from a history where colonialism has decreed that the Orient, India, its languages, its imagery, its very ambience is to be ranked lower than the Occident and its languages and imagery.

I want a character in a book to be true to herself. Rajjo is that, Sunaina is that, babu, dada, and dadi even more so. But that is as long as they speak their own language. When we turn their speech into English, the syntax goes wrong, the vocabulary becomes absurd, and one would have to labour without rest with every single image to get it just right without any guarantee of succeeding. I believe there is no escape from this problem. I believe the problem is exacerbated by the fact that English is used regularly in India and has a wealth of connotations—syntax, vocabulary and image-related. But I think the problem is really bigger. Because, why, otherwise, would it infest not only the speech of characters but everything else in the book as well?

Why cannot one describe a house in English without tremors of dissatisfaction (I crave pardon for sounding melodramatic if I do, but I trust some of my readers at least will share my totally physical reactions to language use)? Because there is an untranslability to *angan*. I can be a woman of my time, with a remarkable postmodernist consciousness, and wander in my angan everyday. But an American woman of the present cannot possibly walk in a courtyard unless she goes to the Cloisters for the purpose. Even as I say this I seem to suggest that the *angan*/courtyard is from the past; if it exists today there is an incongruity, a quaintness. What I would like to say is that there is an orientalist fog we cannot escape whenever we present India in English, if the consciousness of the narrator has been originally expressed in an Indian language. And there is a *modernist* fog, which is the haziness of hierarchy. For those who question whether 'modernity' exists and is a fact, let them simply remember that there is perhaps not a *single* member of the Western world who would hesitate to rank India both as 'non-modern' and 'lower' than a Western country. In the English language, then, all the things of India—courtyards, brass pots, lamps and wicks, bamboo curtains, fruit juices, are not simply things with various properties, they are things that belong to an inferior, non-modern world.

We can accept that there are in Hindi—as in other Indian languages, but I will speak of Hindi from now as a case—some examples of certain genres, say, of detective thrillers, which are written in a way that when translated might read exactly like an English-language thriller, sans all image or ambience of anything non-Western. I don't know. Because I don't know what really is Indian or Western and therefore what may be non-Indian or non-Western. Not because the distinctions and the essences don't exist. But because they lurk everywhere, they defy all definitions, they defeat categorisation, they spill over and stain boundaries.

There are words such as *prasad, charanamrit,* and *gangajal* for which this fact can be explained as part of their religious connotations. But there are others that probably seem to have a religious connotation and this is precisely part of the problem, such as *anchal* or *desi ghee.* If we try to translate 'apron' into Hindi, we come up against a comparable situation: there is no one corresponding word; the word in the original is too multivocal to be rendered by a tight translation; its beauty lies in its complex symbolism, stretching back into centuries, and forward into changing lives, and all this can never be conveyed without a veritable dissertation of footnote. Which, for some of us at least, should have an etymological content, something like the unabridged *OED.*

Much of the time, however, the meaning 'changes' hopelessly. This usage of a term connoting a fixed nature or essence, is permissible only to the 'insider', one who is savouring as her 'own' certain images and expressions, and then, equally as an 'insider' in the other language, is struggling to assert her mastery over language by approximating these images as best as possible. She *knows,* as would any unusual reader who actually sat down to compare the two versions, that the meaning changes even with the best of intentions and efforts. There is then, not so much an essence, as a structure of relationships that gets wrenched loose from the slight adjustment of any of its parts. The new structure may be elegant, convincing, otherwise faultless, but it is *different*. When babu says, '...*nahin karenge bhai*...' (translated evasively by me), there is a complex of sensibilities—class, gender, age, and personal—that cannot be carried over intact into any expression in English. He says *karenge* and not *karunga* (an aspect of class and region), he says *bhai* and not *Sunaina* (gender, age, and personality), and he gives his statement an overall abstractness and passivity that is his personality. This is an exercise that could be prolonged into book length, analysing every nuance of the original for its history, philosophy, and narrative thrust (as in Damsteegt 1997). I do not pursue this line at all because I am not interested in how the author says what she does, or the translator does what she has to, but in *what* the author says and we can know through the translation.

Therefore, interested much more in the content than the form, my discussion is doomed to appear like a fixing or pinning down of the *real* or *actual* intent of the text. The problem with a translation is that it is based on the assumption of non-availability of the original and the corresponding monopoly of the translation to convey the meanings of the text. I see no recourse from this. In this discussion, however, I would like to emphasise *this* hierarchy, of all the hierarchies of discourse that inevitably exist within and surrounding a text. I emphasise that *Mai* in the original, and hopefully in the translation, is not a realistic text, unreflexively privileging one discourse as true, conflict-free, and therefore superior. I hope, further, to position myself in a way that what I am making here are 'propositions' and not enunciations; propositions based on the recognition of the 'stereographic plurality' of the text (Barthes 1971).

~

Then we come to another aspect of translation. We are reading as women, that is, being constructed and constructing ourselves as female readers. We are writing as women, as feminist, postcolonial, in my case, ethno-sociological consciousnesses. But where does this consciousness come from, what is it grounded in?

I can answer for myself. Hindi is my *mother tongue*. For the first time, I realised while doing this translation why the cadences of 'Indian English' sound so natural to me: a mistake, but a natural mistake. *'Mai se zyada ham hi dyorhi men mandrate rahte'* will naturally occur to a Hindi speaker as 'More than mai it was we who kept hanging around the house'. A Brit might say, 'We were the ones who, rather than mai, seemed to be unable to leave the house.' A Brit and maybe some of us Indians who have been trained in schools like Subodh's. The point is not a comparison of Indians' English versus English people's. Professor Higgins confirmed years back that only foreign people can speak correct English because they are trained in it unlike English people. I have two quite other points to make. First, whatever my natural desire in translating might be, I will choose to use correct English because—simply speaking the characters in the novel, as well as the narrator, are all using their language 'correctly' and without a hint of exoticism, quaintness, awkwardness, etc. To do this I have to know this correct English, which only one who has been in the privileged class of Indians with a certain education can be. Second, most such Indians then do not know their own mother tongue as well, either correctly or colloquially. They function, including writing creatively, think, and dream in English.

I am not interested in the merits or demerits of this right now. What I want to puzzle about is, how then do we know this mother tongue (second or third language as it becomes) at all, and what status does it have? It has a peculiar pull, is my claim, for embedded within it is a political commitment known in shorthand as 'mine' and 'my'. Generations of Indians through the 19th and 20th centuries, five to nine by a rough count, have had this experience. Their formal training has been totally in English, and they have picked up their mother tongue on all sides alongside. From their relatives, their servants, the streets, popular events and culture, more elevated arts, the sounds of the world around them. This builds a base and a love, both together the motivation for a politics. Then, with maturity there took place a self-education, and a learning, through books, if not a teacher, of the mother tongue in adulthood.

This was the course followed by me and others I know personally. This translation is infested by a double politics: that which allowed me to have an involuntary knowledge of English *better* than my mother tongue, involuntary on my side and due to the decision of my *mother* and father. And then, in the second turn of the screw, when I understood the implication of this state of affairs, sensed dimly some injustice in the world, and sought vaguely to rectify it by blundering around with some kind of self-education in Hindi. I must note for the record that as a spoken language I always associated it more with my mother than my father. Fathers in general are more educated formally and therefore more fluent in English, which they then try to speak to their children. Apart from English, what my own father spoke was Urdu; what he had studied was Arabic and Persian. I cannot to this day say I have ever seen a Hindi word written in his hand, apart from the shaky *Om Ganeshay namah, Om Lakshamay namah* that he wrote on a new notebook every Diwali puja.

In South Asian history and politics, the sociological position of the mother, and the work of the mother beyond what is stereotypically understood as 'mothering', must be taken seriously. She does not simply nurse and nurture, feed and socialise. She teaches and transmits a language correctly, in this context known as the *mother* tongue, even though, given the capital possessed by

formal schooling, she does this only incompletely. But she builds a
base that the grown child's burgeoning politics can build on.

That the child 'acquires' language through interactions with the linguistic autonomy of a maternal rather than paternal figure' (Gilbert and Gubar 1994: 391) has significance beyond the case of South Asia. Kristeva would argue that the symbolic linguistic order being primarily patriarchal, the maternal can never have a voice within it except through the very structures that repress it. Thus, 'As long as there is language-symbolism-paternity, there will never be any other way to represent this nature/culture threshold, this instilling the subjectless biological programme into the very body of the symbolising subject, this event called motherhood' (Kristeva 1984: 241–42). But my language is more my mother's than my father's, and the obstacles in representation of motherhood are more historical and cultural than eternal or essential.

I feel the need to call my Hindi my mother tongue. Is English, then, a later accretion, the father tongue, the language of formal schooling, career and advancement, formality and reason? Or, even as Thoreau (unwittingly) put it, when those in my position re-discover the mother tongue, is it that 'The one is commonly transitory, a sound, a tongue, a dialect merely, almost brutish, and we learn it unconsciously, like the brutes, of our mothers. The other is the maturity and the experience of that; if that is our mother tongue, this is our father tongue, a reserved and select expression' (Thoreau 1973: 95).

The 'problem' of the mother is also the problem of the 'mother' tongue. And equally insoluble. But equally, I hope, worthy of being pursued.

REFERENCES

Antharjanam, Lalithambika. 1998. *Caste me out if you will*. Translated with an Introduction by Gita Krishnankuthy. Calcutta: Stree.

Bal, M. 1985. *Narratology: Introduction to the Theory of Narrative*. Toronto: University of Toronto Press.

Barthes, Roland. 1989. *The Rustle of Language*. Trans. Richard Howard. Berkeley: University of California Press. Orig. pub. 1984.

de Beauvoir, Simone. 1961. *The Second Sex*. Trans. H.M. Parshley. New York: Bantam.

Benjamin, Walter. 1985 (first published 1968). "On Translation". In *Illuminations: Essays and Reflections*. New York: Schocken Books.

Byatt, A.S. 1991. *Possession: A Romance*. New York: Vintage.

Chandra, Sudhir. 1998. *Enslaved Daughter: Colonialism, Law and Women's Rights*. Delhi: Oxford University Press.

Chodorow, Nancy. 1978. *The Reproduction of Mothering*. Berkeley: University of California Press.

Dalmia, Vasudha, and Theo Damsteegt, eds. 1998. *Narrative Strategies: Essays on South Asian Literature and Film*. Delhi: Oxford University Press.

Damsteegt, Theo. 1997. *Giriraj Kisor's Yatraem, A Hindi Novel Analysed*. Groningen: Forsten (Gonda Indological Studies, VI).

Foley, Douglas. 1996. "The Silent Indian as a Cultural Production". In *The Cultural Production of the Educated Person: Critical Ethnographies of Schooling and Local Practice*, ed. Bradley A. Levinson, Douglas E. Foley and Dorothy C. Holland. Albany: State University of New York Press.

Friedan, Betty. 1963. *The Feminine Mystique*. New York: Dell.

————. 1981. *The Second Stage*. New York: Summit.

Gilbert, Sandra M., and Susan Gubar. 1988. *No Man's Land*, volume 1, *The War of the Words*. New Haven: Yale University Press.

————. 1989. *No Man's Land*, volume 2, *Sexchanges*. New Haven: Yale University Press.

————. 1994. *No Man's Land*, volume 3, *Letters from the Front*. New Haven: Yale University Press.

Greer, Germaine. 1971. *The Female Eunuch*. London: Paladin.

Hutcheon, Linda. 1980. *Narcissistic Narrative: The Metafictional Paradox*. New York: Methuen.

Irigaray, Luce. 1985. *This Sex Which is Not One*. Trans. Catherine Porter and Carolyn Burke. Ithaca: Cornell University Press.

Jacobus, Mary, ed. 1979. *Women Writing and Writing About Women*. London: Croon Helm.

————. 1986. *Reading Woman: Essays in Feminist Criticism*. New York: Columbia University Press.

————. 1995. *First Things: The Maternal Imaginary in Literature, Art, and Psychoanalysis*. New York: Routledge.

Jefferson, Ann, and David Robey, eds. 1982. *Modern Literary Theory: A Comparative Introduction*. London: Batsford Academic and Educational Ltd.

Krishnaraj, Maithreyi, and Karuna Chanana. 1989. *Gender and the Household Domain: Social and Cultural Dimensions*. New Delhi: Sage.

Kristeva, Julia. 1984. *Revolution in Poetic Language*. Trans. Margaret Waller. New York: Columbia University Press.

Kumar, Jainendra. 1980. *Tyag patr*. Trans. Agyeya as *The Resignation*. Delhi: Hind Pocket Books.

Kumar, Nita. 1991. Windows, Education, and Social Change in Twentieth Century Banaras. *Economic and Political Weekly* XXVI, no. 17: WS 19–25.

————, ed. 1994. *Women as Subjects: South Asian Histories*. Calcutta: Stree Publications, and Charlottesville: University Press of Virginia.

————. 2000. *Lessons from Schools: The History of Education in Banaras.* Delhi: Sage Publications.

Lakshmi, C.S. 1984. *The Face Behind the Mask: Women in Tamil Literature.* New Delhi: Vikas.

Marathe, Sudhakar, and Meenakshi Mukherjee, eds. 1986. *Narrative: Forms and Transformations.* Delhi: Chanakya Publications.

Millay, Edna St. Vincent. 1928. *The Buck in the Snow.*

Moore, Marianne. 1967. *The Complete Poems of Marianne Moore.* New York: Macmillan.

Morrison, Toni. 1987. *Beloved.* New York: Knopf.

Ong, Aihwa, and Michael G. Peletz, eds. 1995. *Bewitching Women, Pious Men: Gender and Body Politics in Southeast Asia.* Berkeley: University of California Press.

Preston, James J. 1982. *Mother Worship: Themes and Variations.* Chapel Hill: University of California Press.

Rakesh, Mohan. 1989. *Mohan Rakesh ki sampurn kahaniyan.* Delhi: Rajpal and Sons.

Rice, Philip, and Patricia Waugh, eds. 1989. *Modern Literary Theory: A Reader.* London: Edwin Arnold.

Rich, Adrienne. 1976. *Of Woman Born: Motherhood as Experience and Institution.* New York: Norton.

Rimmon-Kenan, S. 1992. *Narrative Fiction.* London: Routledge.

Schweickart, Patrocinio P. 1989. "Reading Ourselves: Toward a Feminist Theory of Reading". In *Speaking of Gender,* ed. Showalter.

Selden, Raman. 1985. *A Reader's Guide to Contemporary Literary Theory.* New York: Harvester.

Showalter, Elaine. 1977. *A Literature of their Own: British Women Novelists from Bronte to Lessing.* Princeton: Princeton University Press.

————, ed. 1985. *The New Feminist Criticism: Essays on Women, Literature and Theory.* New York: Pantheon.

————. 1985. "Toward a Feminist Poetics". In *The New Feminist Criticism,* ed. Showalter, pp. 125–143; also in *Women Writing and Writing about Women*, ed. Jacobus, pp. 22–41.

———. "Feminist Criticism in the Wilderness". In *The New Feminist Criticism*, ed. Showalter, pp. 243–270.

———, ed. *Speaking of Gender*. New York: Routledge.

Sobti, Krishna. 1967. *Mitro Marjani*. New Delhi: Rajkamal.

———. 1991. *Ai larki*. New Delhi: Rajkamal.

Strathern, Marilyn. 1984. "Domesticity and the Denigration of Women". In *Rethinking Women's Roles: Perspectives from the Pacific*, ed. Do. O'Brien and S. Tiffany. Berkeley: University of California Press.

Waugh, Patricia. 1984. *Metafiction: The Theory and Practice of Self-Conscious Fiction*. London and New York: Methuen.

von Werlhof, Claudia. 1988. "The proletarian is dead: Long live the housewife!". In *Women: The Last Colony*, ed. Maria Mies, Veronika Bennholdt-Thomsen, and Claudia von Werlhof. London: Zed.

Woolf, Virginia. 1957. *A Room of One's Own*. New York: Harcourt.

———. 1967. *Collected Essays*. London.

———. 1978. *Jacob's Room*. New York: Harcourt.

———. 1977. *The Pargiters: The Novel-Essay Portion of* The Years, ed. Mitchell A. Leaska. New York: Harcourt.